ROXY'S
BABY

By the same author
Run, Zan, Run
Missing
Bad Company
Dark Waters
Fighting Back
Another Me
Underworld

CATHERINE MACPHAIL

ROXY'S BABY

BLOOMSBURY

Acknowledgements

A special thanks to Sarah for trusting me to
write Roxy's story, and to Roxy Clark for letting
me use her wonderful name

First published in Great Britain in 2005 by Bloomsbury Publishing Plc
38 Soho Square, London, W1D 3HB

Copyright © Catherine MacPhail 2005
The moral right of the author has been asserted

A CIP catalogue record of this book is available from the British Library

ISBN 0 7475 7042 6
ISBN-13 9780747570424

All papers used by Bloomsbury Publishing are natural, recyclable products made
from wood grown in well-managed forests. The manufacturing processes conform
to the environmental regulations of the country of origin.

Printed in Great Britain by Clays Ltd, St Ives Plc

1 3 5 7 9 10 8 6 4 2

www.macphailbooks.com

This book is for all my children,
with love and thanks

CHAPTER ONE

Roxy crouched in a corner listening to the sounds of Dragon House in darkness. A door swinging shut, the creak of a floorboard. Every sound made her jump. Were they searching for her? She imagined them stalking her from room to room, from floor to floor. They would find her before long. She was shaking with fear. She drew in a deep breath. She would not let her fear take over. She couldn't. She had too much to lose. She had to be strong, to be brave. For once in her life she had to think of someone other than herself.

She had to stop thinking of the fear. Stop shaking.

She had to think of something else.

How did she ever get herself into this situation? She had asked herself that question a thousand times. It was all her own fault. She couldn't blame anyone else. Yet remembering how it all began was almost as painful as what was happening now.

She opened her eyes and tried to focus in the darkness. In her imagination shadows were coming to life, creeping towards her, every shadow a terror.

She tried to forget that they were searching for her. She tried to forget what they would do to her if they found her. She tried to forget that there was a dead body lying just metres away from her.

And the only way to forget, was to remember. Remember home, and family and her life before this nightmare began …

'Where have you been till this time of night!' It wasn't a question. Her mother was screaming at her, not really expecting an answer. 'I've been worried sick!'

Roxy shrugged. 'I didn't realise it was this late. OK!'

'No. Not OK at all. It's one o'clock in the morning, Roxy. You're grounded.'

'You wish,' she said sullenly.

Her mother's eyes flashed with anger. 'Don't you dare talk to me like that.'

She could see that her mother was almost ready to lash out at her, but Roxy knew she wouldn't. Her mother had never lifted a hand to either of her daughters. Still, Roxy took a step back, just in case. There was a first time for everything.

'You show your mother some respect.' It was Paul, her mother's husband, trying to sound as if he could command her obedience. Standing there in a crumpled T-shirt and jeans, looking as if he'd slept in his clothes.

'It's none of your business,' Roxy snapped. And it was true. He was nothing to her.

'Get to your bed, Roxy. Right now.' Her mother almost pushed her up the stairs and Roxy made as much noise as she possibly could, banging her fist against the wall, kicking each step as she went up, anger spewing out of her. She slammed the bedroom door open, not caring if she woke her sister or not. But of course, Jennifer was already awake, sitting up in bed waiting for her, her lips pursed, her arms folded. What was that old saying ... 'nursing her wrath to keep it warm'? That was what Jennifer was doing. Nursing her wrath.

'You don't care, do you?'

Jennifer had her long auburn hair curled up on top of her head. It made her look older than twelve, even in the dark of their room, only dimly lit by the street lamp outside.

'Oh, shut up, you!' Roxy had had enough for one night. She wasn't going to listen to her little sister ...

little sister! That was a joke. Jennifer was twelve going on eighteen. She acted as if she was her mother sometimes.

'You make Mum cry every night and you just don't care!'

Roxy sat at the dressing table and began brushing through her tangle of red hair. Jennifer was having none of that. She leapt out of bed and pulled her round to face her. The brush flew out of Roxy's hands.

'You're going to listen to me for once. You're out every night with your poxy friends. Friends!' Jennifer almost spat the word in Roxy's face. 'They're lowlifes, every one of them. And you hang on their every word. They stay out late, so you stay out late. They say jump and you jump. Goodness knows what they get up to.' Jennifer had tears in her eyes, tears of anger. She sniffed them back, determined not to cry in front of the sister she had come to hate. 'Don't you think Mum's come through enough? She had Dad to look after, and now that she's got a chance for a bit of happiness herself, you start acting like a selfish idiot.'

Roxy jumped to her feet. '*She's* come through enough. Big deal. He was my daddy, and I had to watch him suffer as well. I had to watch him die!'

'So did I,' Jennifer reminded her as she had so often before. 'But I don't make that an excuse for hurting Mum.'

Roxy grabbed the brush from the floor and started dragging it through her hair again furiously. 'Don't worry about her. She's got a new man. Didn't wait too long, did she?'

'She waited long enough,' Jennifer said.

Roxy could never understand how her sister could think that. Two years? Was that long enough to forget Dad?

'You're just making excuses for being nasty and selfish.' Jennifer spat the words out.

In that second Roxy hated Jennifer. 'I'll keep on being selfish.' Roxy said it with determination. I'm going to look after number one. Me! Nobody else is.'

'In my opinion number one is Mum. Not you!'

That really made Roxy sick. 'Of course, Little Miss Perfect's never selfish, is she? She's always too perfect to make mistakes.'

Jennifer lifted her chin defiantly. Her hair was always gleaming, her face shone from her days outside in the fresh air, playing netball, winning races, winning everyone's heart. The Little Miss Perfect daughter every-one admired.

She must be such a comfort to you, Mrs Connor. Such a caring wee girl. Everyone said that. The neighbours, the teachers, her dad's sister, Auntie Val. They all loved Jennifer. Who needed Roxy?

'It's not hard to look perfect next to you,' Jennifer snapped.

Roxy had had enough. She threw the hairbrush at her sister. It caught Jennifer on the eye and she let out a yell as if she'd been shot. She clutched at her face and fell back on the bed.

'Drama queen!' Roxy yelled at her.

'I'll make you sorry for that.' Jennifer leapt towards her. Roxy tried to step aside to avoid her and fell against the mirror. It toppled dangerously, but Roxy was losing her balance too. She grabbed for Jennifer's long hair, gripping it with both fists. She held on as tight as she could, trying to pull herself upright. Jennifer screamed, she too trying to stop herself from falling. Impossible. Both girls tumbled down, tangled up in each other, yelling, shouting, scratching. The mirror went crashing down beside them, splintering, cracking, sending shards of glass flying across the floor.

The light was suddenly switched on. Their mother was there, her eyes red-rimmed from crying. She was wearing her yellow nightshirt with a pig on the front.

'Oh my God! What are you doing!' She stepped towards them and let out a gasp as she put her bare foot on shattered glass. 'You broke the mirror.' She said it to Roxy, only Roxy. She said it as if it was the final straw. 'Seven years' bad luck. Does that mean I have to put up with seven more years of you?'

Roxy gave Jennifer one last punch, and then she ran out of the room. She pushed past Paul, standing on the landing looking confused. He didn't know what to do. He'd not been in the family long enough to know how to handle this.

'Pig!' she screamed at him as she passed, and already she could hear little Miss Perfect consoling her mother with soothing words.

'Don't let her bother you, Mum. We'd be better off without her. I'll buy you a new mirror. It's only a stupid superstition. You'll not have seven years' bad luck. I'll make sure of it.'

Roxy slammed the bathroom door shut. She stared at herself in the mirror. Her hair was long too, like Jennifer's. But Jennifer's was straight and shiny and swung around her like silk. Roxy's was red and wild and unruly. Her eyes had once been hazel bright, but they seemed dull to her now, as if a light had been switched off somewhere inside her. 'Daddy's girl', they had once called her. Now, there was no Daddy to listen to her. Someone else had taken his place. She hated them all. And they hated her.

She suddenly felt sick. She clamped her hands over her mouth to stop herself from retching. They mustn't hear her. They mustn't suspect that there was some-thing else to worry about now, because that would only make them hate her even more. Her mother would never understand and neither would Jennifer.

She could imagine their accusing stares. The very last straw, they would say.

'We'd be better off without her,' Jennifer had said. They had a nice family unit without Roxy spoiling it. And she would certainly spoil it now.

She was going to have a baby.

Someone else they wouldn't want.

Roxy had thought of nothing else for weeks, ever since she suspected she was pregnant. She'd thought about what she was going to do. One thing for sure was that they wouldn't stand by her. They'd had enough of

Roxy. They'd throw her out.

Well, she would go before she'd give them the chance to do that. She wouldn't take their condemnation. She couldn't face telling her mother, or seeing Paul's patronising look, or listening to her perfect sister's accusations.

There was only one thing for her to do. Run.

CHAPTER TWO

Roxy stood in the bathroom holding on to the sink, staring at her reflection. She could see the sweat breaking out on her forehead, little beads of sweat like tiny bubbles. Her mouth was dry. She could still hear her mother crying in the bedroom above her, but Roxy couldn't cry. She was too frightened for tears.

She had only known for sure yesterday, when she'd taken a bus to the far side of town, to a big impersonal supermarket where she hoped no one would know her and she'd bought the pregnancy test kit. She had stood in the toilet cubicle, listening to the other customers outside laughing and talking, while she stood, shaking with fear, praying, actually praying for one blue line and not two. Because she couldn't be pregnant. It was impossible. She'd only done it once, and her friends said they'd done it lots of times and that you never get pregnant the first time. They'd promised her – her friends,

Pat and Tracey and Jaqueline. She could still see their annoyed looks at the party. Still see the boy (though she could hardly remember his face), swaying, hardly able to focus as he waited for her.

'We've all done it, Roxy. Come on, don't be such a wimp,' they had said, teasing her, egging her on. And so, after she'd drunk too much Buckfast, giggled too much and let him kiss her, it didn't seem such a big step. And she so wanted to be one of them; to be like them. Pat and Tracey and Jacqueline didn't seem to care about anything. They swept through life defiantly.

They were her friends.

So she had done it. Once. Could hardly remember a thing about it – except being sick right after. Dead romantic.

But this wasn't supposed to happen. She wasn't supposed to get pregnant.

She was only fourteen.

Roxy had never wanted her mother as much as she did at that moment. What was she going to do?

'Get rid of it!' She could almost hear Pat saying that. If she had confided in her, in any of them, she was sure that would have been their advice. And she was sure she couldn't do that. So she hadn't told Pat or Tracey or

Jaqueline. She had told no one. No one knew. It was her secret.

She could see her fear reflected in the face in the mirror. She was so different from Jennifer. Roxy's hair was a mass of curls, fiery and red and wild. 'Just like you, Roxy,' her mother had told her often. Once she had said it with affection, as if she was proud of Roxy's fire. But lately, it had always been an accusation.

Roxy sat on the bath and tightened her arms around herself, trying desperately to think. She had no other option but to run. Once she could have told her mother. Once, when her dad was alive. Or would she? Maybe when Dad had been fit and well, she might have told her, told her anything. But not when Dad was dying. She wouldn't have told her then. Dad dying would have been enough for her mum to cope with.

Once, she might even have confided in Jennifer. Once, when they had talked and laughed and giggled together.

Now she hated her sister with a passion. Her self-righteous little sister who never did anything wrong.

Her mother and Jennifer hated her now too. So did Paul, though she cared nothing for him. All of them hated her. She didn't belong in this family any more.

'Are you OK in there?' It was her mother, banging on the door.

Roxy opened her mouth. It would only take her a second to say … 'No, Mum, I need you. Help me.' For a split second she was almost ready to open the door, throw herself into her mother's arms.

Not enough time.

'Get you into bed right now! I've had enough of your nonsense tonight. You've got school in the morning, and I've got work.' There was no compassion in her mother's voice. She'd had enough.

Then her angry footsteps pounded into the back bedroom she shared with her new husband. The room she had once shared with Dad. And the door was slammed shut.

When Roxy did go to bed, Jennifer was already sleeping, or was pretending she was. There was no one to confide in. No one to help her. She knew she had to run away, be independent. But where could she go?

She lay in bed, watching the moon hanging in the sky, and tried to figure out what to do. There was no family who would take her in. No handy aunt who had always understood and preferred Roxy. On the contrary, she was sure Aunt Val had always had a soft spot for

Jennifer. There was no darling old uncle in the country who would harbour her and turn her life around. That only happened in books. This was real life, and there was no one she could turn to. So, where could she go?

London. Isn't that where everyone went? There, in such a big city she could lose herself, and in London there had to be places, people who would help girls in her position. All she needed was time to think things through, to work out a plan. But of course, now, time was something she didn't have too much of.

Roxy had once read somewhere that if you were looking for something, by some kind of strange magic it usually appeared in front of you. There was a word for it. *Serendipity*.

Roxy found the answer she was seeking in her hands the very next day. She idly opened a magazine in the girls' cloakroom at school. It had been left there by one of the other girls and she began to flick through it. She caught her breath when she found an article about a place, a house in London, just the kind of place she was looking for. A house which took in runaway girls, looked after them, asked no questions and didn't make them go home if they didn't want to.

There was a photograph of the woman in charge. Thin-faced, with an abundance of iron-grey hair and steel in her eyes. 'Young girls run for many reasons. It's not for me to judge, just help them.'

London. Mayflower House. Jessica Jones.

The answer to her prayers?

Roxy ripped the page from the magazine and stuffed it into her rucksack. This was like a message, she was sure of it. If she still had doubts about running away they disappeared when she read that article. It was telling her what she had to do, telling her where she had to go.

She began to make her plans. Even so, every morning that week she still prayed she might be wrong. That the pregnancy kit she had used had been faulty. And every morning after Paul and her mum had gone off to work she was retching in the bathroom. She was pregnant all right. Nothing could change that. By Friday, she had no choice. She had to leave.

When she spoke the words to herself it all sounded easy and sensible. 'You're running away, you know where you're going. Someone is going to help you.' But as she packed her rucksack on that last night she had never wanted to stay so much.

Everyone had gone out for the evening. Her mum and Paul had been invited to an evening reception at a wedding. Her mother looked so pretty in a scarlet dress and Roxy couldn't take her eyes off her as she stood in the living room, laughing and sharing a glass of wine with Paul. She even kissed Roxy. Her mother could never stay mad at anyone for long, even her errant daughter. She gave Roxy a hug as they were leaving and for the first time in ages Roxy didn't pull away from her. All she wanted to do was to hug her back, to hold tight on to her.

'Don't be late tonight, Roxy. Please. I'm trusting you.'

'I won't,' Roxy said, as if it was true, and she watched from the doorway as they climbed into a taxi and waved goodbye to her.

I'm never going to see her again, Roxy kept thinking. I'll be out of her life tonight for ever.

Still the tears wouldn't come. I must be as hard as nails, Roxy thought, or as strong as steel. She much preferred being strong as steel. She wouldn't think about it. Too much thinking was bad for her, and anyway, there were too many emotions inside her fighting for her attention.

She took money from her mother's stash in kitchen. She wanted to write a note saying she would pay it back, but she probably wouldn't. Jennifer was at a sleepover and wouldn't be home until the next day. How would she feel when she knew Roxy had gone? Guilty? I don't think so, Roxy thought, she'll probably just be glad to get the bedroom to herself.

She pictured her mother, waiting up for her coming home, striding backwards and forwards across the living room, as she had done on so many nights recently. Watching at the window for Roxy running up the street or getting out of a taxi. She would grow angrier and angrier but it would be morning before she would raise any alarm. She would phone the friends she so disapproved of, and it would take perhaps all day before she realised that Roxy was with none of them and might not return this time. And by then, Roxy planned to be in London, melted into the crowd.

Alone.

She would have to get used to being alone.

She stood in the dark hallway of her house for a long time remembering. Remembering the happy times here. Her dad sneaking presents into the front room on Christmas Eve. Her tenth birthday party, before Dad became ill, when they'd presented her with a bike. She remembered the sad times too. How often Dad was rushed to hospital from here, how often she and Jennifer had sat on the stairs waiting for the phone to ring to tell them how he was. And she remembered the angry times. The night Mum had brought Paul home and Roxy had known, she had simply known that this was the one who was going to take her dad's place. No matter what she said, or what she did, he was going to become part of the family.

Yet, at that moment as she listened to the sounds of the house she had grown up in, she would have done anything to change things. To be able to stay here, safe and secure. Especially now.

She was afraid. Afraid to go. But even more afraid to stay. Let's face it, Roxy, she thought, they'd put you out anyway when they found out your dark secret. Roxy, the black sheep, spoiling the image of the happy family.

Roxy – all alone.

She looked at the big clock above the fireplace. It was almost time to go for the train that would take her to Glasgow, where she would catch the overnight bus to London. The red eye, they called it. The article from the magazine was wedged tight into her rucksack. At least she knew where she was going.

'Goodbye, house.' She said it softly and waited for a moment, almost as if she expected an answer. Then she quietly closed the door behind her and was gone.

CHAPTER THREE

Roxy slept all the way to London. She hadn't thought she would. She'd been sure the fear, the uncertainty about her future, would keep her awake and alert on the long dark journey. Yet, she slept.

She woke just as the bus was coming into the outskirts of London. People waking up, pavement cafes opening and tables and chairs being prepared for the springtime customers.

She'd been to London only once before. Just after Dad had died her mum had taken her and Jennifer for a weekend treat. Staying at a big hotel, going to a show.

Now, here Roxy was, back again, and this time there was no money for hotels or shows or fancy restaurants.

For the first time in days she didn't feel sick, and she took that as an omen. She'd done the right thing. She even ate breakfast in a typical London 'caff', the only place that was open so early in the morning. It was filled with lorry drivers and taxi drivers munching on hot bacon rolls and hugging mugs of steaming hot tea and all talking like the cast of *EastEnders*.

After her second cup of tea she noticed that the eyes of the fat waitress were on her too often and for too long. It was time to move on. Roxy unfolded the article from the magazine and laid it flat on the table. She read it over again, and it sounded too good to be true, this haven waiting for her. Mayflower House. This woman, Jessica Jones. Too good to be true. 'You're so cynical, Roxy,' her mother was always telling her, because she was always suspicious of other people's motives. 'They must be after something,' Roxy would say, and her mother would always reply, 'There are a lot of nice people in the world.'

Well, there were a lot of nasty people too. Was Jessica Jones one of them?

She asked one of the drivers sitting at the next table which line she should take on the Underground. Not the waitress, because she already looked too suspicious, staring at Roxy from under a dyed blonde fringe.

He answered, spluttering breadcrumbs all over her table. 'You get the Piccadilly line, darlin', that's the one you want. Know where you're going, love?'

'My aunt's, I'm down here for a holiday,' Roxy said at once, with assurance and a broad smile, as if it was the truth. She was a good liar, always had been.

She felt the waitress's eyes follow her as she left the caff and she deliberately beamed a smile at her, catching her off her guard. The waitress smiled back, her fat face like the dough of an unbaked bread roll. 'Have a nice day,' she called out, as Roxy stepped out into the sunshine.

'You too,' Roxy called back.

She hated the Underground. Hated the crowds and sounds and the smells. Hated the swoosh of wind that came out of a tunnel with every train as if it was going to carry her off. It was rush hour and every seat was full. There was hardly any room to stand up. She was constantly afraid she wouldn't be able to fight her way out of the crowd and she would miss her stop. When she reached ground level and saw the sky again she took a moment to rest and breathe in fresh springtime air. Then she was ready to move on. She bought a street map from a pavement stall, and followed her route street by street. Her legs were aching and she was exhausted by the time she reached her destination.

At last there it was. Mayflower House. It stood right

in the middle of a sweep of houses in a half moon crescent. They looked like the old Georgian buildings in Edinburgh. The kind they used in fog-shrouded melodramas, where husbands tried to drive their wives mad, or bodysnatchers sneaked out into an eerie street looking for their next victim. The houses here all looked run-down, and that disappointed Roxy. These houses could have been beautiful, but paint flaked from the graffiti-stained walls and windows were boarded up or had grilles in front of them. Some of the houses looked as if they had been turned into grotty flats, with filthy once-white net curtains draped across the windows.

The front door of Mayflower House was flanked by two chipped columns. The wood on the high windows was breaking up and the stonework was crumbling. She thought of her own neat little terraced home, the front garden with the pot plants and the climbing wisteria and honeysuckle, once her dad's pride and joy. For a moment, hurt by the memory, Roxy felt on the verge of tears, but she sniffed them back. That was then, she told herself. This was now. No going back.

The brightly shining brass plate on the column restored her confidence. Someone at least took care of *this* house. The front door was lying open, letting the morning sunshine flood into the hallway. A girl was arranging some flowers in a vase and Roxy stood watching her for an age. She was very thin, with pale fair hair. Her mouth was hanging open as she concentrated on her task. She doesn't realise anyone's watching her, Roxy thought, or that mouth of hers would be shut. Almost as if she had heard her, the girl turned, saw Roxy and her mouth snapped closed.

'Are you coming in?' she asked. She saw Roxy hesitate, and she came forward. 'Come on in.' She smiled, but Roxy didn't smile back. She didn't move.

'My name's Doreen,' the girl said. 'I work here. Mrs Jones is out but she'll be back soon. Fancy a cup of tea?'

Roxy stepped into the shabby hallway. It was brightened up by the flowers and multicoloured throws draped over a couple of sofas against the walls. Doreen followed her gaze. 'I know, it doesn't look much, but there's never enough money to do it up. That's where Mrs Jones is now, trying to get some more sponsors. Run away from home, have you?'

Roxy blushed, but Doreen didn't seem to notice. She hardly paused. 'I ran away too, long time ago. Now I work here. Trouble at home?'

Roxy didn't answer her and Doreen shrugged. 'Tell

me to mind my own business. I'm so nosy it's unbeliev-able. I'm always getting into trouble for it.'

Roxy said softly. 'Aye, trouble at home. That sums it up.'

'From Scotland, are you? Well, so far there's been nothing on the telly about you, so have you just left home? Just a couple of days ago, eh?'

She is right, Roxy thought, she is nosy. She was glad that only a few moments later a woman stepped into the hallway. Roxy recognised her right away as the woman in the article, Jessica Jones. She was thinner than she'd looked in the photograph and her grey hair was untidy and pulled back with clips. She put her briefcase on the hall table and stared at Roxy. She did not at that moment look like a woman who was going to welcome her with open arms.

Doreen immediately began telling all. 'She's from Scotland, Mrs Jones, she's just run away. Trouble at home, she says. Young, isn't she?'

Mrs Jones silenced Doreen with the merest lift of her eyebrow. Then she turned back to Roxy. 'You read the article in that magazine, didn't you?' She didn't wait for Roxy's answer. Jessica Jones pursed her lips in annoyance. 'I knew I should never have agreed to that interview. Since that article I have been inundated with silly girls who have one quarrel with their parents and decide to run. And where do they run ...? Here!'

'I've not just had one quarrel with her ...' Roxy began to say, but her voice broke in a sob. Maybe it was the sob that made Jessica Jones's eyes soften, the line of her jaw become less hard.

'I'm sorry. I'm not usually this judgemental. Did you come down on the night bus?'

Roxy nodded.

'Then I think before we have a really good talk you need a good sleep in a comfortable bed.' She turned to Doreen. 'Get a bed ready upstairs. I'll have a cup of tea with ... what is your name?'

Roxy almost told her, held back at the last minute. 'Ro — Rosemary,' she muttered.

Doreen didn't want to leave them. She fumbled with the flowers as Mrs Jones led Roxy into another room. She closed the door before she said a word. 'Try not to tell Doreen too much of your business, Rosemary.' She sat on the sofa and motioned Roxy to sit beside her. 'Now, why exactly did you leave home?'

Roxy thought about what to tell her. If this woman was going to give her the chance to stay then she couldn't tell her the truth, not all of it. 'Trouble at home,' she said.

'Lots of girls have trouble at home, they don't run away. Your parents – your mother and father – they'll be worried about you.'

Roxy shook her head. 'No. They won't. They don't want me any more.' She looked straight at Jessica. 'Anyway, my father's dead. I have a stepfather now.' She let the implication of that sink in. They were bad to her. *He* was bad to her.

Jessica nodded very slowly as if she was mulling that over. 'Have they been violent towards you? Have the police ever been involved?'

Roxy shrugged. 'No. Not the police. But I can't stay there any more. And I can't go back. You won't make me, will you?'

It took a long time for Jessica to answer. 'I would never make you go back. But since that interview, this is the first place the police seem to look for runaways. And if they come to me, I can't lie about you. You must see that.'

Roxy saw her dreams of staying here fading fast. But if she couldn't stay here ... where could she go?

'The article said you always helped, you never tell on anyone.'

'I believe you're under age,' Jessica said. 'That makes all the difference. I do help all I can, but I will not break the law. I'm sure you could get something sorted out once the police are involved. They wouldn't make you go back either.'

Roxy drew in a deep breath at the mention of the police again. Anything but that. 'You're going to tell them I'm here?'

Jessica said nothing for a moment, till Roxy asked her again.

'I'm sorry, Rosemary, but if the police are looking for a runaway under-age girl I couldn't possibly not inform them you're here.'

Roxy had to know at least that she was safe here for the present. 'Please don't tell them about me now. Not today. At least give me until tomorrow.'

Finally, Jessica smiled, her pale thin lips drawing back and tightening her skin. She looks as if she's had a lot of worries, Roxy thought.

'I'll wait till tomorrow, I promise that. I want you to rest without worrying about that at least.'

It was as much as she could ask for. Roxy sank back on the sofa. She was suddenly very tired.

Jessica took her arm gently. 'Do you really want

some tea?'

Roxy shook her head, told her about breakfast at the cafe. Jessica nodded. 'Then I think you should get to bed now. You're tired. Sleep, Rosemary, that's what you need.'

Roxy was sure she would never sleep again, not till she knew she was safe. 'You promise you won't tell anyone I'm here. Not yet.'

Jessica smiled again. It seemed sincere, but Roxy had never trusted sincere smiles. 'Sleep, Rosemary. We'll talk when you wake up. But for the moment you have my word that no one will know you're here.'

CHAPTER FOUR

It was dark and the house was quiet when Roxy woke up, and for a moment she was totally disorientated. She felt as if she had been asleep for hours. Where was she? She expected to open her eyes and see Jennifer asleep in the bed across from her. But it wasn't Jennifer who lay there. It was the girl, Doreen, letting out gentle snores.

What was she doing here in this house, with strangers? Why wasn't she at home with her mother and her sister? Safe. Secure. She imagined she could hear her mother rattling about in the kitchen, almost picture her with a towel wrapped around her head, just out of the shower, fixing breakfast for them before drying her hair.

One phone call, and they would surely come for her. I could be there now, Roxy thought. Why don't I just go home?

In that instant, almost as if she was being told the

answer, her stomach began to heave. She sat up, desperately trying to remember where the bathroom was in this strange house, hoping she could make it in time. She jumped out of bed and ran for the door.

When Roxy stumbled back into the bedroom Doreen was awake, sitting up in bed, waiting for her.

'You all right?' she asked.

Roxy slipped back into bed before she answered her. 'Fine.' She pulled the covers up to her chin, shivering. She just wanted to sleep again now.

Doreen lay back down, resting her head on her hand. She still watched her intently. 'You're going to have a baby, aren't you? Know the signs.'

Roxy peered at her in the darkness. Could she trust her? 'You won't tell on me, will you?'

Doreen muffled a giggle. 'You won't be able to keep it a secret for long.'

That was true. Time was against her. 'That woman, that Jessica, she'll help me, won't she?'

Doreen hesitated. Roxy could make out her eyes now, her face. Doreen was thinking hard. 'She's really nice, Jessica, don't get me wrong. But she will send you back. You're under age, you see, and you're pregnant. Of course she's going to inform the authorities. She won't think she's got a choice. She's a typical do-gooder. They do good, but only up to a point.'

Roxy felt like crying. She'd come all this way and she was no further forward. She'd be sent back, like an unwanted package. Perhaps Jessica Jones had lied to her and had already phoned the police and they were on their way, wailing towards her in police cars, on trains, in planes, hurrying to get her.

'I won't go back,' she said, almost to herself. 'I can't go back.' Yet now it seemed she didn't have anywhere else to go.

Doreen got up from her bed and crossed to Roxy's. She sat beside her and clasped both her hands. 'I don't know if I should tell you this ...'

'Tell me what?'

Doreen hesitated. 'Maybe I know people who can really help you.' Her voice was almost a whisper, as if she was afraid someone might be listening. 'People who definitely won't send you back. I know that for a fact. Real do-gooders. They've helped lots of girls in your situation.'

'Who are they? How can I find them?' Roxy was suddenly desperate to get away from this house, sure that at any moment, her mother, Jennifer and Paul could come charging up the stairs, accusing her of hurting them, being selfish, not caring about anyone but herself. Then it would begin all over again. Only worse this time because of what she carried inside her.

'Can you get in touch with them?' she asked Doreen.

Doreen put an arm round her shoulders. 'Don't look so worried. I'll contact them.'

'Today,' Roxy said. 'It has to be today.'

Doreen didn't disagree with that. 'I know.'

Roxy lay down and tried to sleep again, but it was impossible. She was enveloped in fear. She had thought she could feel safe here, but she didn't. If anything, she was more afraid. Why had she believed that stupid article? She would have been safer going anywhere but here. When Jennifer Jones informed the police, her family would know she was in London. They would find her. But now, she had hope again. These people Doreen knew, she prayed they would be able to help her.

She managed to fall asleep again, but as soon as she heard sounds coming from downstairs she was up and dressed. She shook Doreen. 'When are you going to phone them?'

Doreen opened one bleary eye. It was as if she was trying to remember, then she smiled. 'Soon as I'm up. I promise.'

Then she stretched and closed her eyes again. 'Just give me another hour.'

Roxy went downstairs. So far she had seen no one else in this house. It had been quiet when she arrived and here, in the early morning sunshine, apart from the noises coming from the kitchen, it was still quiet. She had slept for a long time.

There was a delicious smell of hot bread wafting towards her and Roxy suddenly remembered just how hungry she was. Eating for two, a voice murmured. She imagined the baby inside her for the first time, a real person. Calling out for food. 'Feed me!'

She scratched out the thought. It was impossible that she, Roxy, had a living, growing baby inside her. She still couldn't take that in.

'You certainly slept well.' It was Jessica, standing at the living-room doors, watching her as she came downstairs. Roxy nodded her answer. 'That's obviously what you needed,' Jessica said.

Jessica Jones was wearing a long cream cardigan and a long cream skirt today. Colour coordinated, Roxy thought. It all blended in with her long cream face.

'We didn't wake you last night. You were in such a deep sleep. You must be starving now.'

Roxy breathed in the heavenly smell of the hot bread. She nodded.

Jessica took her arm and led her through the house and into the dining room. There was a long table with a motley assortment of chairs and benches.

'You sit there,' Jessica said. 'I'll get us some breakfast.'

Roxy wolfed down the freshly made bread and hot tea. Nothing had ever tasted so good. She just hoped she didn't spoil things and spew it all up again.

Jessica was watching her closely.

'I'm sixteen, you know.' Roxy tried to say it with assurance, as if even she believed it was the truth.

She didn't fool Jessica Jones. 'More like fourteen, Rosemary. Though I'm sure Rosemary isn't your real name either.'

'I'm not going back. You don't know how bad they were to me.'

Did she feel guilty telling such lies? No. Not if it was going to save her from being sent back.

'The authorities won't send you home without

checking things out. Under those circumstances, they'll look into all your accusations.'

Roxy snapped at her. 'That's what they always say. They'll look into it. Then they just leave me there … and it all starts again.'

What would start again, she wondered? But already, Roxy was imagining an alternative truth where she'd been slapped and beaten and abused. She stared at Jessica. 'Have you told them I'm here yet?'

'Not yet,' Jessica said. 'I told you I wouldn't, didn't I? But I will have to soon. You're too young. It's dangerous on the streets.'

'It said in that article that you protected girls like me. You wouldn't tell on them. It was all lies.' Roxy couldn't keep the disappointment out of her voice.

Jessica shook her head. 'I do protect girls like you. I give you a place to sleep, I try to help you get somewhere to live, and work, find out all the benefits you're entitled to. But you're under age, and I can't take the responsibility for leaving you in London alone.'

Roxy saw all her dreams of staying here fading. Her only hope now was Doreen and these people she knew. 'What are you going to do now?'

'I'll speak on your behalf, I promise.'

'Just give me another day,' Roxy said, standing up. 'Before you do anything. That's not too much to ask, is it?'

Jessica stood up too. She tried to hug her, but Roxy stepped back, embarrassed.

'What if we go to the police together, Rosemary? In the afternoon. It's better getting it over with.'

Roxy said nothing for a moment, then she managed to give her the sweetest smile she could muster. 'OK,' she said, 'if you think that's best.'

Her smile was a lie. All the time she was thinking, You old bat, and I thought you'd help me.

The dining room had begun to fill up by this time with girls waking up and coming downstairs for breakfast. No one seemed to notice Roxy. New faces must come and go every day. She supposed that in a way every face was a new face in this house. She scanned the room for a sign of Doreen. Finally, she appeared at the door and Roxy ran to her.

'Well, did you talk to them?'

'Sure did. Just off the phone to them.' Doreen filled a bowl with cereal. 'They'll meet you this morning. There's a coffee shop a couple of streets away. They'll meet you at eleven o'clock.'

She grinned at Roxy. 'Don't look so worried. The Dyces are wonderful people. You're sorted, Rosemary.'

CHAPTER FIVE

It was easy to sneak out of the house without anyone seeing Roxy. It was as if she was invisible. It made her realise how insignificant she was in this house of runaways. Today she was glad to be invisible. The last thing she wanted was for Jessica Jones to see her leave, realise she had no intention of coming back, and stop her.

Doreen had given her directions to the coffee shop where she was to meet Mr and Mrs Dyce. It was easy enough to find, up one of the back streets where there was more litter and broken windows and drab buildings. Coffee shop was a rather grand title for the dilapidated cafe that stood on the corner.

As Roxy stood at the door she was suddenly afraid. Here she was meeting up with strangers, expecting them to help her. She was frightened of what was ahead. The unknown. Was she ready for it? Not for the first time she thought how stupid all this was. She could just go home now. Head for the bus station. Be back in her own bed tonight.

If her family would take her back, that is.

Were they worried about her? Or just glad to be rid of her?

Just glad to be rid of her, probably. That thought decided her. She took a deep breath and went inside.

Nobody seemed to notice her. Only the untidy waitress in the corner glanced her way, and that for just a second. Roxy scanned the tables looking for the Dyces. A woman sat reading a newspaper and smoking. Roxy studied the headlines to see if there was any mention of her going missing. There was a story about a football player who'd been arrested, and a pop singer who'd just won an award. Nothing about her. Yet. At the next table, another woman fanned the cigarette smoke away furiously. A young couple, both looking ridiculous in matching red berets, sipped coffee and muttered sweet nothings to each other. Could they be the Dyces? No. Of course not. They looked too young, and too stupid. She wouldn't go anywhere with them. She'd never trust them.

There was no one else here. She was almost ready to leave when a hand gripped her elbow.

'Rosemary?' The voice was a whisper in her ear.

Roxy swung round. A thin woman, her hair looking newly permed, was smiling at her. 'You are Rosemary?' she whispered again. It was as if her voice was always a whisper. 'We've got a table over there.' Roxy followed her glance to a dark corner of the cafe, beside a side entrance. All she could see at the table were a pair of chubby hands folded together. The rest was hidden by the wall. 'You go and sit down with Mr Dyce. I'll get us some tea. Is tea OK?' Her voice never rose above a whisper. There was something reassuring in that.

As Roxy drew closer to the far table the hands grew into arms and then a body and a face. Whatever she was expecting, she certainly wasn't expecting this. She was looking into the face of Santa Claus. Round, with apple-red cheeks and a trim white beard.

'Is it you, my dear? Is Mrs Dyce bringing the teas?' He looked beyond her to the counter. 'Come, sit down.' He patted the seat beside him. Roxy sat down nervously.

'I'm Mr Dyce,' Santa Claus said. 'I don't really like this place. It's frequented by some very strange people.'

None stranger than you, Roxy was thinking.

He leaned towards her. 'I don't suppose Rosemary's

your real name, but you'll tell us when you're ready. Ah, here comes Mrs Dyce with the tea.'

He looked vaguely excited at the prospect. Not just tea, but scones too. Hot and oozing with butter.

'You had them warmed up, dear?' Mr Dyce sounded delighted, as if his wife had just discovered penicillin. Mrs Dyce lifted one of the scones and put it on his plate. She even cut it in half for him. He beamed at her, and she beamed back at him. Love's young dream, thought Roxy, feeling sick.

Then Mrs Dyce turned to Roxy. 'Now, my girl, tell us all about yourself and let's see if we can help you.'

The lies flowed easier this time. She told them of the hard time she'd had at home. The classic evil stepfather – she almost made Paul sound like a dangerous psychopath. That was a joke. She remembered the first time Paul had tried to dig in the garden. He'd come in, terrified after ten minutes, because there were 'too many bees. I'll get stung out there.'

This time Roxy added an extra dimension which she thought was rather clever.

'He brought his own daughter into the house too … and they prefer her to me.'

They listened quietly. Well, not quite quietly. She'd

never heard anyone eat as noisily as Mr Dyce did. Or make so much mess. He spluttered scone all over the table and Roxy couldn't take her eyes off the currants lodged in his beard.

'Delicious scones. Who would have thought it in a place like this?' He sounded so pleased with himself that Roxy found herself smiling at him.

She still felt sick. The scones didn't taste so delicious to her, or the tea. Everything tasted funny just now.

His wife only tutted. 'Look at the mess you're in.' And she began picking the currants out of his beard and placing them on his plate. Roxy was disgusted. She'd never love anybody that much. When Mrs Dyce was finished she squeezed his cheeks with her fingers and grinned at him.

They're acting like teenagers, Roxy was thinking, and yet there was something touching about the obvious affection they had for each other.

It reminded her suddenly of her dad, and the way he would wink at her whenever Mum would moan at him over something he'd done. A secret wink, just between them.

'Look at the mess you've made of my kitchen!' Mum would shout whenever he'd try his hand at some cooking. And Dad would wink and grin, just the way Mr Dyce did.

Roxy felt her eyes fill with tears. It was so stupid to feel like this. It wasn't like her.

Mrs Dyce saw the tears and reached out and touched her face. 'Doreen told us some of the things about you. But I don't know what she told you about us.' She raised an eyebrow and Roxy noticed that one long hair trailed from her eyebrow to her cheek.

'She said you'd help me.' In the end that was all that mattered, that they would help her.

Mrs Dyce drew in a long sigh. 'The first thing I'm going to tell you, or advise you, is to go home. Things probably aren't half as bad as you think.'

Here we go again, Roxy thought, no one really wants to help. They just want to send me back. 'No! Can't do that. You don't understand.' Her voice became as soft as a mouse's whisper. 'I'm going to have a baby.'

She knew by their reaction that this wasn't news to them. Doreen had filled them in on this too.

'You want to go somewhere safe, with us? Now?' Mr Dyce said softly.

All her mother's warnings of never going off with strangers rang in her mind. 'But why are you doing this? Why should you want to help me?' she asked them.

Mrs Dyce sighed. 'I was in your position once, a long time ago. My parents made me go to a home … for unfortunate girls.' She paused as if the memory still hurt. 'They made me have my baby adopted. I wasn't able to have any more.' At that Mr Dyce clutched at her hand. 'So I decided that I would never let that happen to any other girl if I could help it.'

'We have a nice house in the country,' Mr Dyce said. 'There are other girls there. You could come with us today … it would give you time to decide what you want to do.'

'You won't tell on me … even though I'm under age.'

Mrs Dyce shook her head. 'We won't tell. Though we would still advise you to go home.'

Roxy felt better, in spite of her misgivings. If they were advising her to go home, then they must have her best interests at heart, surely? It would be OK. She was sure of it.

'Mr Dyce will go and get the car. You wait at the front door, I'll just go and make sure I've paid for all this.'

Mr Dyce left by the side door and as Roxy waited

outside the cafe she began to feel tired and sleepy. Being pregnant was exhausting. Too much on her mind, too much happening.

It was almost five minutes before Mr Dyce's car appeared at the corner, and by that time all Roxy wanted was to sit down and rest. He drove a wood-trimmed Morris Minor estate, and that seemed like an omen too. It was her dad's favourite car. 'You can always trust a man who drives a Morris Minor,' he would say, laughing. She was sure that car was a message. A message from her dad saying she was doing the right thing.

Mr Dyce beckoned her over. 'I got lost. It's all one-way streets here. Don't tell Mrs Dyce.' And he winked at her, and there was her dad again.

Roxy climbed into the back seat. A moment later Mrs Dyce appeared from the side entrance and climbed into the front seat. She turned and smiled at Roxy. 'I know you must be worried. We're perfect strangers and here you are going off with us in a car. Normally, I'd be telling you never to be this stupid. But these are strange circumstances that you're in. On the streets, anything could happen. At least, I know you'll be safe with us. Me and Mr Dyce.'

Roxy didn't answer her. Her mind was in a turmoil,

and she ached all over. She felt her eyes grow heavy as she leaned back and watched as the car sped out of London.

CHAPTER SIX

They were fascinating to watch, this Mr and Mrs Dyce. She fussed around him like a mother hen, picking flecks of dust from his jacket, patting down his hair, constantly touching him. He drove like some old duffer who had just passed his test. Twenty-eight miles an hour, weaving across the white line and fiddling with the air conditioning, winding the windows up and down, trying to find the right channel on the radio.

Both of them wanted to listen to some play. 'You don't mind, do you, dear?' Mrs Dyce turned and asked her.

Roxy didn't mind. She was tired, felt her eyes heavy with sleep, but she was trying desperately to stay awake. They could listen to anything they wanted, as long as it wasn't the news. Because the news just might be about her, and she might have to listen to her mother, tearful, begging her to come home – or would she? Maybe she wouldn't even bother with any kind of appeal and deep down that was what frightened Roxy more than anything else.

She was scared too that if they heard her mother on the radio, they would know she'd lied – that her whole story was lies, and then, what would they do? Put her out, dump her here on the streets of London?

'Where is it we're going?' she asked sleepily.

'We have a lovely house in the country. In its own grounds. Secluded, plenty of fresh air, no one to bother you there. Just what you need for a growing healthy baby.'

'Doesn't that cost a lot of money?'

'We have money, and no one to spend it on.' Mrs Dyce tugged at her husband's ear fondly. 'Isn't that right, dear?'

'This is a dream come true for us,' he replied.

Roxy was finding it hard to understand. Doing all this for her, for other girls like her, and wanting nothing in return? No one was this nice, surely? This sincere? Everyone wanted something. So what was it they wanted?

Yet, here she was in their car, and as she watched them, they seemed so ordinary, so like everyone's favourite aunt and uncle. She had a sudden moment of disorientation, thinking that this wasn't happening. It was all a dream, she wasn't really here, she couldn't be. And soon it would turn into a nightmare. When they reached this lovely house in the country – was there really such a place? – they would turn into monsters and the house would be some dark Victorian prison.

'You look tired, dear,' Mrs Dyce said softly. 'Why don't you try to sleep?'

Roxy had promised herself she wouldn't sleep. No matter how tired she was. She wanted to watch where they were taking her, see exactly where this idyllic house was situated. But she couldn't help it. It was as if her eyes were being dragged shut with weights. She leaned back in the seat. She would only close them for a moment, she told herself, because she wouldn't, couldn't sleep. She had to see where they were going.

It was Mrs Dyce shaking her that woke her up. 'We're here, dear,' she was saying.

Roxy's mouth was dry and she felt sick. She could hardly open her eyes, they were so heavy. She looked around. The car was on a long winding gravel drive with a wide sprawling lawn on either side. A man was

56

working at some hedging and he was watching her closely. Mr Dyce acknowledged him with a wave.

'Stevens,' he said. 'Our odd-job man.'

Roxy looked at him. Odd was just the right word for him. She turned away from his stare to study the house.

'Like what you see?' Mr Dyce asked her.

What was there not to like? Roxy thought. The house was like something out of *Country Life* magazine, the kind that she would sift through in the doctor's surgery. An impressive four-storey building built of grey stone, with high windows and attics. Curtains fluttered from the open windows on the first floor, baskets hanging from archways swayed in the breeze, roses curled round the front door.

'It's a big house,' was all she said.

Mr Dyce opened the car door to help her out. 'We don't use it all. We've closed off some of the rooms. It's too big for just me and Mrs Dyce.'

Now was the moment when the stupidity of what she was doing hit Roxy full blast. She was here alone, no one knew where she was. She had been so stupid to come here. Her eyes darted about in a panic, looking for a place to run, and she saw Stevens again, a dark sinister figure watching her. There were three of them, and only her. Were they all in on it?

In on what?

She didn't even know what she was thinking. She only knew that suddenly she had a really bad feeling that she'd done the wrong thing … again.

Mr Dyce held out his hand patiently to help her. Mrs Dyce was standing beside them. Roxy felt trapped. And it was too late to run.

Shapes like dark phantoms began to weave in front of her eyes. The last thing she remembered was seeing the floor of the car coming up to meet her.

CHAPTER SEVEN

A girl was smiling at Roxy when she opened her eyes. It took her a moment to remember where she was. Was she safe? Had she been rescued? Then Mrs Dyce's smiling face appeared behind the girl and she knew nothing had changed.

'Are you feeling OK now, dear?' Mrs Dyce bent towards her, felt her brow. 'You fainted. I think it was the heat. Are you ready for a nice cup of tea?'

Roxy said nothing. A feeling of utter hopelessness was closing in on her, like an icy fog. Her eyes followed Mrs Dyce as she walked to the door.

'This is our Anne Marie,' Mrs Dyce said. 'She'll be sharing this room with you.'

It seemed to Roxy that her voice faded to an echo, as if she was moving far into a deep dark cave. As Mrs Dyce opened the door, Mr Dyce was dancing about outside impatiently. 'Is she OK? Can I see her?'

'Now, now, dear.' Mrs Dyce patted her husband's hand. 'Calm down. She's fine. She just needs some rest and some hot tea. I'm about to organise that.' She looked back at Roxy and smiled. 'Come along, now. Let's leave Rosemary with Anne Marie. Let them get acquainted.'

The door closed quietly and they were alone – Roxy, and the smiling girl who was Anne Marie. Roxy's eyes moved around the room. It was bright and freshly painted, white walls and buttercup-yellow curtains fluttering at the window. The beds had white throws over them, and the lamps had buttercup shades that matched the curtains. The smell of freesias filled the room from the vases of flowers that stood on the window sills and the dressing table. It was a nice room, comforting. Roxy blinked and looked at Anne Marie. She was older than Roxy, but not much. Seventeen perhaps, eighteen at the most. Her hair was thick and black and cut short. She was a little plump, but Roxy thought that was just because of the baby. She was probably too skinny before.

Anne Marie was watching her just as closely. 'You must be scared,' Anne Marie said. Her accent was soft and Irish. She didn't wait for Roxy's answer. 'I was scared too when I first came here. Didn't know what to expect. Thought they,' she nodded to the door as if the Dyces were still standing there, '"had ulterior motives".' She sketched inverted commas with her fingers and giggled. 'Well, I've been here three months and nothing could be further from the truth. With the Dyces, what you see is what you get. They are just lovely people. A bit on the daft side.' She made a face and Roxy found herself smiling back at her. 'Let's face it, they must be more than a bit daft to finance all this. But their hearts are in the right place. They really do want to help us.'

Roxy leaned up on her elbows, and with the effort she realised how weak she felt. 'But why? What's in it for them?'

Anne Marie came and sat on the bed beside her. 'Do you know, I think we've all grown so cynical we don't think decent people, honourable people exist any more. But they do, and they're called the Dyces.'

Roxy sat up. She was beginning to feel better. No more dark phantoms in front of her eyes, only an intense hunger. 'How did you get here?' she asked.

'Came over from Ireland,' Anne Marie said. 'Planned to have an ...' She hesitated, as if she couldn't even bring herself to utter the word. 'Planned to have an abortion over here.' For the first time her smile slipped and she looked almost sad. 'Couldn't go through with it. The Dyces found me, took me here. They would have stood by me whatever decision I might have made, they said. But I want my baby now. So much.' She breathed in deeply as if she was sending her life-giving air straight down to that baby. 'The Dyces have been so kind to me.'

'But how did they find you?' There couldn't be another Doreen, could there?

'It was a nurse at the hospital where I went to have the …' Again she couldn't say it. 'Anyway, she saw how upset I was and she put me in touch with the Dyces. Mrs Dyce is a midwife too, you know. So we're well looked after here.' She waved her hands about as if they had talked enough about her. 'Now. What's your name?' She didn't give Roxy a chance to answer. 'I know it isn't Rosemary. You might as well tell me your real name. It won't matter here.'

So she did. Glad to admit her name at last. Her name was the only thing she had left of her past.

'Roxy,' Anne Marie repeated. 'I like that. And you're from Scotland. Don't tell me where, it doesn't matter.'

She grinned. 'Oh, we're very cosmopolitan here. Girls from all over the world, would you believe? We're lucky to get in here, let me tell you. Mostly, the girls they help are like illegal immigrants, or girls who are on a work permit from countries like … Romania, or Albania. And now that they're pregnant – they can't work.' She began to laugh. 'It's like the United blinkin' Nations in here.'

She was making Roxy laugh, this Anne Marie. She could see that and she just carried on with her blethering. 'Mrs Dyce says, here we're all one, citizens of the world, all with one problem: our little babies. And that's where she helps.' She pinched at Roxy's cheeks. 'You're looking better already. We've landed lucky here, Roxy. So let's make the most of it. And you know, after the baby if you want to go home, you can. Mrs Dyce will make sure of it. She'll arrange that too, if you want it. But what would you want to go home for? Look at this place.' Anne Marie waved round the room proudly, showing it off. 'I lived in a dump back home. Why would I want to go back there?'

But Roxy hadn't. She was thinking of her own bedroom, hers and Jennifer's, with the music centre and the computer and the TV, and her cuddly toys and her posters. Not as tidy as this, but much … much more cosy.

She couldn't think about that. Couldn't bear it.

'When's your baby due?' she asked Anne Marie.

Anne Marie patted her bump. 'In just three months' time. And that's the other lovely thing about the Dyces. If you want to keep your baby, they'll help you do that. Get you organised with accommodation, set up all the benefits you're due. But if you want to get it adopted, they help you do that too. And then you know the baby is going to a decent family.'

'It all sounds too good to be true, Anne Marie.' And it was. Roxy was too cynical to believe all this. It was heaven.

Anne Marie flashed her a smile. 'Aren't you the hard one? Well, I'll give you a week here, and you'll believe it all right. Roxy, it is too good, but it's still true.'

It was hard not to smile back at Anne Marie, to take everything she said as the truth. 'What about you, Anne Marie, are you going to keep your baby?'

There was no hesitation in Anne Marie's answer. 'Keep my baby? Definitely. I'm so looking forward to it, Roxy.' She stroked her bump affectionately. 'This is the first time in my life that I'm going to have someone who loves just me.'

CHAPTER EIGHT

Mrs Dyce brought the tea in on a tray. On it were two mugs and a jug of milk and a bowl of sugar. 'Getting to know our Anne Marie? That's good.' She laid the tray down on the table between the beds. 'I'm going to have to leave you two girls. I've got so much to do. Anne Marie will bring you down to lunch.' She adjusted a picture on the wall. Roxy had seen one like it before: a girl in a bar, staring out at them, her reflection behind her. Then Mrs Dyce smiled at them both and left. Roxy didn't say a word until the two girls were alone again.

'How can they afford to do this?' She was looking around at the fresh paint, the bright furniture. She bounced on the bed. 'Good mattresses. How? Come on, they've got to have an angle.'

Anne Marie shrugged and poured milk into her tea. 'She's very rich, I think. Or maybe he's the one with the money. I don't know. They haven't got any children of their own. So this is how they spend their money. Are you complaining?' Anne Marie suddenly sounded annoyed. Her face creased in a frown. 'I don't care how they afford it. They can go out robbing banks at the weekend for all I care. I just thank God, His holy mother and all the saints, that they *can* afford it.'

Her face broke into a smile again. As if it wasn't used to frowning. Smiling came as natural to Anne Marie as the moon at night.

'Won't your parents be looking for you, Anne Marie?' Wouldn't they miss that smile, Roxy wondered, in their house every day?

'They won't care tuppence, Roxy. Take my word for that. I'll never go back there. Especially after he's born.' She patted her bump.

'Or she?' Roxy said. 'It could be a girl.'

Anne Marie shook her head. 'No, I know it's a boy. I had a scan and they told me. Aidan, I'm going to call him. It's a good name, isn't it, Roxy?'

'It's a lovely name, Anne Marie.' A thought occurred to her. 'They take you to the hospital to have your baby?'

'They don't have to. We have everything we need

here at the house. There's a delivery room too, in one of the wings.' She waved a hand vaguely in another direction. 'A doctor comes once a week to check us out, and we have our own resident nurse too. That's Mrs Dyce. Oh, fair play to them, Roxy. They look after us awful well.'

Too well, Roxy was thinking. Too good to be true. She was too afraid to relax in case this was some awful charade and suddenly the walls would tumble down, and there would be no yellow curtains, no beautiful grounds. There would only be her and Anne Marie caught in a dark menacing lie.

Anne Marie's giggling brought her out of her reverie. 'Oh, Roxy, I can see already the type you are. Trusting nothing or no one. Just enjoy. Be grateful. You'll feel better when you meet the rest of the girls at lunchtime. There's only about a dozen of us. Most of them are foreign, can't speak a word of English. It makes communication very difficult. There's a couple of them you should stay well back from, but I'll keep you right about them. But once you've met us all, and got to know us, you'll see there's no tricks, no mystery. We've just landed lucky.'

The dining room was bustling with activity when

they went downstairs. A couple of girls, dark-skinned, quiet girls, were laying tables. Another two were already sitting at their places reading magazines. Three were clattering about in the kitchen. All of them were in different stages of pregnancy. All of them, as far as Roxy could see, much further on in their pregnancy than she was.

'This is Roxy,' Anne Marie called out without any warning to Roxy. 'She's only just arrived.'

Roxy grabbed her arm. 'You told them my real name!'

'Doesn't matter here, Roxy. No one's going to send you back if you don't want to go.'

There was an echo of greetings from the girls, waves from the ones in the kitchen.

'My! You're a young one!' A brash blonde who had been sitting at the table came across to her. Roxy was a bit annoyed by that. It seemed to her that they were all young. None looked older than eighteen, except per- haps this blonde.

Anne Marie put an arm around Roxy's shoulders. 'That's why we have to look out for her. She's scared. It's her first day here.'

Roxy resented that. She wasn't scared. There were

other words for what she was feeling – apprehensive, suspicious, wary – but she didn't say any of this. All she said was, 'You do your own cooking?'

'On a rota system.' Anne Marie led her to a table and pulled out a chair for her. The blonde stood watching her. 'Three are assigned to making a meal each day, and the next day's team does the washing up. It's a good system,' Anne Marie said, as if it was her idea. 'A very fair system.'

'And there's no getting out of it,' the blonde snapped. Then she laughed loudly. 'I should know. I tried everything. Nothing works. Not even the old "I'm having a baby" routine. Unfortunately, everybody's having a baby in here.'

'That's Babs, by the way.' Then Anne Marie whispered, just loud enough so all the girls could hear, 'But we call her Boobs. You can see why.'

'Boobs' went into a raucous fit of laughter at that, and by the time they were all eating Roxy was laughing too.

'We have to do the cleaning too,' Babs told her.

So that was it. Cheap labour. Roxy tried to imagine them all on their knees scrubbing all the rooms in this massive house.

'Oh, don't listen to a word she says,' Anne Marie said. 'We keep our own rooms clean, make up our own beds, and take our turn of the bathrooms and the kitchen.'

A small voice piped up from the end of the table. 'Anyway, they don't use the whole of this house. Only this one small part for us.' The small voice belonged to a girl who had a big horsey face that didn't suit that small voice at all. 'They really do look after us in here, Roxy.'

'That's Agnes,' Anne Marie whispered, softly this time. 'She's a bit of a bad 'un, as they say. I'll be glad when she goes.'

Roxy giggled into her tea. 'Agnes?' she whispered back. 'You'd think she'd have enough problems with a name like that.'

'Sssh!' Anne Marie tried to shut her up, but she was giggling too.

'I mean,' Roxy went on, 'bad girls don't have names like Agnes. Bad girls have names like –'

Anne Marie interrupted her. 'Like Roxy?'

'Yeah, like Roxy.' Roxy laughed so loud Agnes turned to look at her. 'Are you two going to let us in on the joke?'

Anne Marie didn't answer her, instead she indicated a dark girl sitting beside Agnes. 'Have I introduced you to Sula, Roxy? She doesn't speak very much English. She's Albanian.'

Roxy nodded to Sula and she nodded back. Sula had the loveliest brown eyes Roxy had ever seen. But Roxy's eyes were drawn to the tattoo on her arm – a cobra wound round her upper arm as if it was crawling towards her neck. It gave Roxy the creeps.

'Love her tattoo,' Roxy said sarcastically.

Anne Marie laughed. 'I think it's supposed to ward off evil or something. Blinking awful, isn't it?' But still she smiled at Sula.

Ward off evil. Well, so far it hadn't brought much luck to Sula, Roxy thought, pregnant and alone in a strange land, and she wondered what her story was. Everyone had a story here, she thought.

'Hello Sula,' Roxy said.

Sula smiled. 'I go home.'

Babs turned to Roxy. 'That's just about the only English she knows. And she says it all the time. "I go home." She would drive you potty.'

Sula still smiled. She seemed to know there was no real criticism of her in Babs's tone. Babs leaned across the table and touched her hand. 'That's right, Sula. I go home.'

Sula smiled even wider. Her teeth were off-white and crooked. 'I go home,' she repeated.

Anne Marie told Roxy in a soft voice. 'Sula's an illegal immigrant. She was brought here to work, but she didn't fancy the kind of work she had to do, and luckily for her, the Dyces found her – brought her here. But she's awful homesick. Aren't you, pet?' Anne Marie smiled across to Sula, who was watching them intently, knowing they were talking about her. 'And now all she wants to do is to go back to her mother. Have her baby at home in Albania. And do you know what!' Anne Marie paused dramatically as if she was daring Roxy to disagree with her. 'The Dyces arranged that too. They're sending her back home safely. Don't ask me how! Those two could perform miracles if you ask me anything. Sula's going home.'

Going home. Roxy lay in bed that night, watching the moon as it hung in the sky, a full fat moon.

'No matter where you are in the world,' her dad used to say, 'when you look up at the moon, just remember I'll be looking at the same moon and thinking of you.' He hadn't known he wouldn't be here long enough to look at the moon with her tonight. Was her mother looking at the moon tonight? Or Jennifer? Were they thinking about her? Imagining her in some drug-laden den, sleeping rough, alone and homeless?

She snuggled further under the covers and felt quite smug. Bet they'd never in their wildest dreams think she'd be curled up in a cosy bed, after a full meal, with people looking after her.

Too good to be true. The words were never far from her mind. She pushed them back. Like Anne Marie said, she should just enjoy.

She'd show her mother, and Jennifer. She didn't need them. She could do it on her own. When she saw them again, if she saw them again, she would be completely independent. Looking after herself, and her baby. Her baby. No, she couldn't, wouldn't think of anything real growing inside her. She pushed the thought of a baby far back in her mind.

She closed her eyes. Tired again, so tired. But she couldn't sleep. Something was keeping her from sleeping. Some thought.

There was something missing. Something that should be here – and wasn't.

She had almost drifted off when she realised what it was.

Where were the babies?

CHAPTER NINE

Roxy was sick again next morning. Sula heard her in the bathroom and came in and knelt beside her, soothing her brow with her cool hands.

'Better?' she asked, smiling.

Roxy leaned back against the tiled wall, exhausted. She nodded. 'When you go home?' Roxy asked her, saying it as simply as she could. Not sure if she could understand even that.

It took Sula a minute to answer her, as if she was turning the words over in her mind, translating them into her own language. She held out her hands. Roxy's eyes were drawn again to that tattoo. When Sula moved it was as if the snake moved too, as if was already winding its way ever closer towards her face. It gave her the creeps.

She was almost sick again looking at it. Sula was counting out the days on her fingers.

'Eight days,' Roxy said, and held out her fingers in exactly the same gesture. 'Happy?' she asked, pointing at Sula. 'You, happy?' She beamed her a smile.

Sula's smile was answer enough. Then, she asked Roxy. 'You go home?'

Roxy didn't need to think about it. 'Never,' she said, shaking her head. And she meant it.

Everyone pitched in at breakfast, making their own toast and tea, pouring cereal into bowls, drinking orange juice out of cartons. They sat chatting at the table or wandering out through the French windows into the garden. The morning was already warm, hinting at another scorcher of a day. It was only May, but the weather held the promise of a long hot summer. Roxy took her cereal and went outside. She found Anne Marie sitting on a bench, admiring the view over the gardens. To Roxy, it seemed the view went nowhere, only past the lawn to high grass and trees, and beyond … a mystery.

'You were up early,' Roxy said to her. Roxy herself had gone back to bed after being sick.

'Since Aidan came into my life,' Anne Marie patted her stomach, 'he will not let me have a lie-in.'

Roxy sat beside her. 'I wish I knew where we were,' she said.

Anne Marie shrugged. 'South of England some-where. Does it matter?'

'Aren't you curious?'

'Not particularly,' she answered.

'Won't they tell us if we ask?'

Anne Marie began to laugh. 'Questions, questions, questions, Roxy. Can't you just enjoy the fact you're safe?'

Anne Marie had been here for weeks, Roxy thought, and nothing had happened to her. Care and attention were all she had received. TLC, tender loving care, she called it. So why should Roxy herself not trust all this?

'So what's on the cards for today?'

'After breakfast we'll go and look at the rota, see what chores we've been allocated.' Suddenly, Anne Marie was laughing again. She had a nice laugh, like the warble of a bird. 'You should see your face, Roxy. Shock! Horror! Don't worry, they're not going to send us down the mines to dig coal. We're only expected to do a bit of light cleaning, washing, ironing, that sort of thing.'

She made Roxy laugh. And she remembered too

what had been bothering her last night. 'By the way, there don't seem to be any babies here. Why is that?'

'You know, the very same thing occurred to me when I first came here. I asked Mrs Dyce, and she said that what used to happen after the girls had their babies was that they would keep them here till it was time for them to move on. But that got really distressing for the girls who had decided to have their babies adopted. So now, once you have your baby, you're both whisked away to another house, where all the mothers and babies go.'

Roxy thought about that. 'They have another place?' She knew she sounded incredulous.

'Yes, another place. I think it's really wonderful of the Dyces, not wanting to distress any of us. They're wonderful people.'

Too good to be true. The words leapt into her mind unbidden.

It seemed that Anne Marie could read her mind. 'Too good to be true? Is that what you're thinking? Have you never heard of Mother Teresa? She did the very same thing out in India, and they said she was too good to be true – but she was true, Roxy, and never anyone deserved to be made a saint more … apart from the Dyces, of course.'

Then she gave Roxy a gentle push and they were laughing again. Still laughing when Mrs Dyce came round the side of the house dressed in gardening clothes and behind her, head down and looking surly, was the odd-job man Roxy had seen when she arrived. Stevens. He looked even scruffier today, in a wrinkled shirt and a battered felt hat.

Mrs Dyce stopped to talk to them. 'How did you sleep, Roxy? Well, I hope. I'll want to have a little chat with you later today. Just filling you in on things here, though I'm sure our Anne Marie's done all that already.'

'Our Anne Marie,' she always called her. There seemed to be a genuine fondness for the Irish girl, Roxy thought.

'She's been great,' Roxy said truthfully.

Mrs Dyce touched Anne Marie's cheek. 'I'm going to miss her.'

Anne Marie patted her bump. 'Still got a while to go yet, Mrs Dyce.'

Mrs Dyce beckoned the odd-job man with her finger. 'Come along, Stevens. I'll show you where I want you to put my rhubarb.'

The girls had to stifle their giggles when she said that, but Mrs Dyce didn't seem to notice. She moved off and Stevens walked after her. But as he passed Roxy he lifted his eyes to look at her. And what he saw seemed to cloud his face with anger. She felt herself drawing back from him. He stopped for a second, staring at her, then he shook his head disapprovingly. He seemed to have to drag his eyes away from her face and she was glad when he moved off and disappeared into the shrubbery with Mrs Dyce.

'He gives me the creeps,' Roxy said.

'He gives us all the creeps. Have you noticed his fingers?'

Roxy hadn't.

'They're like chubby little maggots. They look as if they have a life of their own, as if he'd pulled them up out of the soil and if they touched you they'd eat you up.'

She wiggled her fingers at Roxy, who fell back in a pretend swoon on the bench. 'I'll keep back from him and his maggoty fingers.'

'He certainly couldn't keep his eyes off you,' Anne Marie said.

'Yeah, why was he looking at me like that, as if he hated me?'

'Probably because you're so young, Roxy, and you

look it. We've never had anyone as young as you here before. He probably thinks you're a bad lot.'

In the afternoon Mrs Dyce came to get Roxy for their 'little chat'. She led her into the living room to a couple of shabby chairs in a corner. Roxy had expected to go into their office, through the door marked PRIVATE. She had only seen that door open once. Had only time to see a cluttered desk, a swivel chair and a filing cabinet, before the door was pushed closed.

'Their private apartments,' Anne Marie had told her that morning. 'Sure they have to have somewhere private they can go to if they want to get away from all of us.'

That door also led to the delivery room, where the girls were taken to have their babies, she had explained.

'Can I see the delivery room?' Roxy asked Mrs Dyce as they sat down.

'Time enough for you to see it when you're going to have your baby, Roxy,' Mrs Dyce said softly, but her tone cut off any more questions about it. Roxy. Now it seemed her name was no secret to anyone, thanks to Anne Marie.

'Now, you're going to need more clothes as you get

bigger. We have plenty for you to choose from. Anne Marie will show you where they're kept. We've got wardrobes full of maternity trousers and skirts and dresses. You're bound to find something to fit you.'

Second-hand clothes. At home she would have died of embarrassment if her mother had tried to get her to wear anyone else's cast-offs.

'We don't have a lot of rules and regulations here, Roxy. But there are certain ...' Mrs Dyce hesitated, searching for the right word, '*guidelines* we would like you to abide by. For instance, we would prefer it if you stayed within the grounds. There's nothing nearby, it's all farmland, and you could easily get lost.'

Roxy thought about that. 'You mean, we can't get outside at all? Not even for a run in the car?'

Mrs Dyce smiled. 'I think you'll find there are plenty of grounds for you to wander in, and in your condition you won't be able to wander far anyway.'

So far and no further, Roxy was thinking.

'Where exactly are we anyway?' Roxy asked.

Mrs Dyce smiled again 'You don't really need to know that, Roxy. If you decide to go home ... and you're free to go whenever you choose, it's safer for the other girls if you can't tell exactly where you've been.

You can understand that, can't you?'

Roxy nodded, but she still wasn't satisfied.

'You'll learn as you go along, Roxy, that everything we do here is for your own good, and the good of the baby.'

Roxy's chores for the day, if they could be called that, were to tidy the living room, and give it a dust and a vacuum. As she worked alone in the living room, the house seemed unnaturally quiet. She could hear some girls laughing upstairs, hear their voices carry into the still, hot air outside. Roxy switched on the television. Perhaps, she thought, there might be some news of her disappearance, though she could hardly bear to think how she would feel if she saw her distraught mother on the screen at some kind of news conference.

Nothing happened.

She pressed every button on the remote control, then did the same thing on the television itself, but no picture appeared. There was only a screen full of snow.

Babs wandered in from upstairs, fanning herself with a tea towel.

'Babs, the television isn't working.'

'No, it won't,' Babs said casually. 'It only works for

videos and DVDs. You can't get any programmes on it.'

'Can't they get any reception here?'

'They think that if we heard any news it would only worry us. You know, maybe seeing bombs going off or murders "might harm the little babies".' Babs did a fair impersonation of Mrs Dyce's husky voice. '"And we can't have the little darlings coming to any harm, can we?"' It didn't seem to bother Babs. 'Who wants to hear the news anyway? Doom and Death, that's all there is. I suppose it's sensible when you think about it. As long as we've got plenty of videos, and lots of CDs, I couldn't care less.'

A little 'guideline' Mrs Dyce had forgotten to mention.

Yet perhaps it was sensible. Everything they did was thoughtful, for the good of the girls, and their babies.

So why did she still feel that somewhere, deep inside her, a warning bell was ringing?

CHAPTER TEN

Yet, as one sultry day followed another, that warning bell grew fainter. Roxy found she was enjoying herself. The morning breakfasts were fun, sitting outside in the sun, with Anne Marie, eating cereal, drinking orange juice, watching planes fly overhead.

'We must be close to an airport,' she said to Anne Marie one morning as they watched one fly low above them.

'We're on a flight path anyway,' Anne Marie agreed.

'But which airport?' Roxy looked at Anne Marie. 'Don't you ever wonder exactly where we are?'

But Anne Marie didn't. 'You question everything, Roxy. Were you this much trouble at home?'

And she had to admit that she was.

Their chores were never too heavy, just as Anne Marie had told her, and amazingly, even Roxy almost enjoyed them. She had caused mayhem at home, refusing to tidy her and Jennifer's room, leaving heaps of dirty washing lying on chairs or in corners. Here it was different. She didn't have her mother's constant nagging, or her sister shouting her disapproval at her. In fact, here, because she was the youngest, she was treated in a special kind of way. Looked after as if she was the baby of the family.

In these first days she hardly thought of her mother, and when she did it was defiantly. One day she would be able to tell her how well she, Roxy, had done without them. Did she think of her mother crying, worrying over her? Let her cry, she thought. Though half of her was sure her mother wouldn't shed a tear. Glad to be rid of her and have only Little Miss Perfect left in the house. At times, it almost felt as if she was at boarding school, in one of those novels where the girls packed into each other's dorms at midnight, telling stories, eating midnight feasts, laughing.

All that was missing at these midnight parties, according to Babs, was alcohol. 'They could allow us alcopops at least.'

Anne Marie threw a pillow at her. 'Bad for the baby, stupid!'

And they were never allowed anything that was bad

86

for the baby.

A doctor came every Wednesday. An Austrian, Anne Marie informed her. Roxy would never have been able to tell just from his accent. He could have been anything, from German to Dutch to Russian. To Roxy, he was just a middle-aged man with a fuzz around his chin, as if he was trying to grow a beard and failing miserably.

Anne Marie laughed when she told her that. 'You're so funny, Roxy.'

Funny? No one had ever accused her of that before. Anne Marie laughed even louder when she mimicked his thick accent. '"Yourrrrr bebe will be a perrrrfect specimen. You will produce many fine bebes."'

'Did he actually say that?' Anne Marie asked through her giggles.

'He did. I nearly died. So did Mrs Dyce.' She jumped forward. '"Oh, Doctor, for goodness sake. She's not a battery hen."' Roxy's Mrs Dyce impression only made Anne Marie giggle all the more. 'I told him I didn't want to produce this one. I'm not planning producing another for a very long time.'

They both fell back on the bed laughing. 'Anyway, why can't they get a proper British doctor?' Roxy realised that had been bothering her all day.

Anne Marie, of course, had an answer. 'It can't be easy for them to get doctors they can trust, Roxy. What they're doing here for us has to be a secret. Otherwise the police, social workers would be swarming all over the place. You'd have to go home, so you would. They can hardly phone up the village doctor and ask him to make a house call.'

Everything about this place was secret, undercover, and Roxy didn't like those words. Yet, she did understand the necessity for all this secrecy. Otherwise, where would Anne Marie be, or Agnes or Babs? Or, especially, Roxy herself.

And Sula, who wanted home.

As the day of Sula's departure drew near she grew more and more excited.

'We're going to have a farewell party for her,' Anne Marie whispered to Roxy one day in the kitchen. It was their turn to make the evening meal – spaghetti Bolognese, crusty bread, salad.

'When?' Roxy asked.

'She leaves on Friday morning, so we'll have it after dinner on the Thursday.'

Mr Dyce strolled into the kitchen just then. Roxy had seen little of him since her arrival. He was always working in his office. That room marked PRIVATE. A couple of times she had seen him driving away in his Morris Minor. He always had a vague and distant look about him, Roxy thought. He had that look now, smiling, but at no one in particular.

Anne Marie was as fond of him as she was of his wife. She ran to him and slipped her arm in his. 'I'm telling Roxy that we're having a party for Sula before she goes home.'

'Yes. Wonderful idea. Is it a secret?'

Anne Marie squeezed his hand. 'Yes. So no telling.'

He drew his fingers across his mouth as if he was closing a zip and then he winked. 'Tight shut.'

'How are you getting her home?' Roxy's question took Mr Dyce aback. She could tell by the way his eyes darted towards her. 'I mean, she hasn't got a passport or anything.'

He looked at Roxy, still smiling. 'With great difficulty,' he said. 'My, you are the inquisitive one. Always asking questions.'

Roxy would have asked more but Anne Marie interrupted. 'Sula's so near her time, Mr Dyce. I wish you could persuade her to stay till after the baby's born.'

Mr Dyce finally drew his eyes away from Roxy, and even though he was still smiling, why did she feel it was only with his mouth? 'We tried, Anne Marie, but she just wants to go home.' He lifted his shoulders in a shrug. 'What can we do?'

'The Dyces must know a lot of people,' Roxy said after he'd gone shuffling out into the garden. 'People who can get Sula back to Albania without a passport.'

Anne Marie shook her head. 'Look at you, still the suspicious one. The Dyces would move heaven and hell to help any one of us. Haven't you realised that yet? Heaven and hell.'

I'm being silly, Roxy told herself later, as she sat eating her spaghetti and listening to the chatter round the table. She'd been here for days and had been shown nothing but kindness. So what if they couldn't listen to the television, or leave the grounds. Those rules had been put there to protect them. Everyone else accepted that. Why couldn't she?

She was like a little boat that had been caught in a terrible storm, and had found, by accident, a safe haven. She still couldn't believe her luck. She would wake up tomorrow and find herself lying in some homeless shelter, hungry and alone.

Why couldn't she just enjoy what was happening? Why did these suspicions keep pounding in her mind, like waves on a harbour wall?

CHAPTER ELEVEN

Sula knew nothing about the party. Her command of English was so poor that the other girls could talk all round her about it and she didn't pick it up. The foreign girls, in spite of the language barrier, were brought on board to help, blowing up balloons, pinning up banners. They each had a job to do. Babs was in charge of making the punch; non-alcoholic. She complained about that bitterly, adding, 'I asked that weirdo Stevens to get us some booze and do you know what he said?'

'He said, "No"?' giggled Anne Marie.

'Not just your ordinary "no". He said, "It is more than my life's worth."' She looked around them all in disbelief. 'Can you believe this guy? It's more than his life's worth? What are they going to do? Kill him? Dismember him, bury him under the rhubarb? Just because he gets us a bottle of sparkling wine?'

They all laughed, and yet the words chilled Roxy.

More than his life's worth? It was a strange thing to say, surely? She would love to have the nerve to talk to this Stevens, even though his appearance – she pictured his maggoty fingers – gave her the creeps.

'Couldn't you sneak into the village yourself?' Roxy asked Babs.

Babs stuck out her belly. 'With this lump? I couldn't "sneak" anywhere. Anyway, what village? We're in the middle of nowhere here.'

'Doesn't that bother anybody but me?' Roxy looked around them. 'Why can't we know exactly where this place is?'

Babs only shrugged, but she answered for the rest of them. 'Couldn't care less. As long as they feed me, water me and give me a bed, this place can be on the moon for all I care.' She laughed raucously and punched one of the Asian girls who was trying to blow up a balloon. 'What about you, Sanja? Bet you don't care either.'

Sanja only looked at her, the balloon hanging from her lips. She smiled. Some of the other girls turned to look too. It occurred to Roxy that they must feel so alone here. They all spoke different languages, and none of them spoke English. It was as if they each lived in their own little world, not really understanding what was going on.

Anne Marie said, 'You know why we can't go into the village, Roxy, so don't start getting suspicious again. Think about it. If one of us goes into the village and we're recognised, this whole place, this whole operation would be put in jeopardy.'

'You know some wonderful big words, Anne Marie,' said Roxy. '"Jeopardy", I like that.'

'Well, I for one have no plans to go into any village.' Babs looked around them all. 'Come on, I can't be the only one the police are looking for?'

Roxy saw Agnes's eyes shoot to the floor. She was on the run too, but not from family, from the law. 'It was only shoplifting. It was the assistant's own fault, she shouldn't have got in the way. I only pushed her.' She defended herself in her squeaky little voice, as if they had all accused her. She almost shouted. 'It wasn't my fault.'

For a moment no one said a word. It was Anne Marie who broke the uneasy silence. 'Where's Sula?'

'Mrs Dyce took her for a walk round the grounds,' Agnes said. 'Just to keep her out of the way, really.'

'Roxy, watch out for her coming back. Agnes, you get the cake ready.'

Roxy stood at the open French windows. The night was still and warm with the scent of roses drifting through the air. It was almost idyllic looking out over the gardens, watching the tall grass sway in the light breeze, breathing in the scents of early summer. She listened to the girls laughing and giggling and felt a warmth for them too. So what if they were petty criminals. They all had secrets. Hadn't she some of her own? Here, they were all in the same boat, and she felt a togetherness with them she hadn't felt with anyone for a long time. Roxy was almost happy – almost. There was still a niggling doubt that this was all going to come to an abrupt end. That in the end there would be a price to pay. That she would have to pay the piper.

'Does Sula's family know she's coming back?' Roxy was asking no one in particular.

It was Babs who answered her. 'She's written to her family. Mrs Dyce posted it.'

'You know, it's hard to believe that someone like Sula with hardly any English and so quiet would want to come here by herself and look for work.'

Anne Marie was already pinning up another banner. CONGRATULATIONS, it proclaimed. 'But she wasn't alone, Roxy,' she said. 'She came here with her boyfriend.'

Babs patted her belly. 'The sprog's dad.'

'He dumped her as soon as he knew she was pregnant.'

'Ratbag,' Babs spat out.

'So, her parents didn't know about the baby, but they're still happy to take her back now?' Roxy was thinking aloud, not really asking anyone.

'Parents usually do. Forgive you anything to get you back.' Anne Marie laughed, but there was a sadness in her voice. 'Unless you've got parents like mine who couldn't care less.'

Would Roxy's mother forgive her, as Sula's had? she wondered. But she dismissed the thought almost immediately. Why would she want to go back there anyway? Hadn't she landed on her feet? Enjoy the moment, Anne Marie kept telling her. So she would. This was luxury. These girls and Anne Marie were her family now.

And Mr and Mrs Dyce her loving parents?

Suddenly, Mrs Dyce appeared through some shrubbery with Sula hanging on to her arm, whispering softly to her.

'They're coming.' Roxy called out. ' Is everything ready?'

They closed the windows and drew the heavy curtains shut, making the room almost dark, and then they pressed themselves against the walls and tried not to giggle. Agnes waited in the kitchen with the cake at the ready.

Roxy stood in a gloomy corner, waiting. She could hear Mrs Dyce's voice outside, moving closer. Murmuring softly, though the words were indistinct. Could Sula understand? Or was she just so excited to be going home she would listen to anything?

The door opened at last and the curtains opened with it. The setting sun streamed in with a fanfare of burnt orange. Sula walked in first, her face puzzled. She looked around, just as the kitchen door opened and Agnes stepped into the room carrying the cake, with the candles already lit.

Roxy stayed back, watching all their faces. Sula immediately began to cry, covering her face with her hands. Anne Marie reached out and pulled her into a hug, then she began to cry too. Even Babs managed a tear, wiping it away dramatically. 'This is ruining my make-up,' she was saying.

Agnes was trying desperately to squeeze one out. Crocodile tears, Roxy's mother would call them. Phoney as a three-pound note. Roxy couldn't cry. It just wouldn't come. She looked around the other girls and her eyes finally fell on Mrs Dyce, and there she was, watching Roxy closely. She wasn't crying either. She wasn't smiling. It was as if she knew what Roxy was thinking, and didn't like it. Then her gaze moved back to the girls and it seemed to Roxy that her eyes were as cold as ice.

It was a great party. They ate the cake and drank Babs's punch and they all got so giggly that Roxy began to wonder if Babs had indeed found some alcohol to put in it. She said so to Anne Marie.

'It's our mood. A good mood, a good laugh, it's better than alcohol any day. And a happy ending, Roxy.' Her eyes went back to Sula, sitting on the carpet, her face glowing as Babs tried to explain in sign language that she must write to them.

'Sula's got her happy ending.' Anne Marie said it wistfully, wishing for her own. 'Don't you just love happy endings, Roxy?'

Loved them, Roxy thought. She just didn't believe in them.

Mrs Dyce stayed for most of the party and only stood up to go when they began to clear the plates and glasses away.

Roxy found that annoying. 'Why does she stay? Can't she see we're just young girls and we want to be alone, to party on down? We can't even talk with her here.'

Anne Marie, as always, stuck up for her. 'If it wasn't for her, none of us would be here. Where would you be, Roxy? She's like a mother to us.' To make her point she crossed the room and linked her arm in Mrs Dyce's.

Mrs Dyce patted her hand and smiled. 'I'm trusting you, Anne Marie, to get this lot to bed. Sula has an early start in the morning.'

With that she crossed to Sula and kissed her brow. 'Tomorrow, Sula.'

Sula beamed up at her. 'Tomorrow.'

They crowded into Sula's bedroom before she went to bed. They all had gifts for her. Anne Marie had given her a holy medal, Babs a little bundle of pot pourri, Agnes had made her a special card. The only one who didn't have a present for her was Roxy.

'You've only been here a week, Roxy. No one expected you to get a gift,' Anne Marie told her.

Sula looked around them all. Her eyes were filled with tears. She muttered something in her own language, over and over again. And though they understood nothing, it was clear what she was saying. They were her friends, and she would never forget them.

CHAPTER TWELVE

They never saw Sula again. By the time Roxy was up next morning, Sula had gone, her bed lay stripped and bare. Her pathetic knick-knacks had disappeared from her bedside table.

'It's as if she's never been here at all,' Roxy said to Anne Marie. The thought bothered her more than she could explain. They were eating breakfast outside in the sun, sitting on a rustic wooden seat that had seen better days. It was a late May morning, already bursting with heat and sunshine.

'Her memory lingers on,' Anne Marie said, laughing as she stuffed an orange segment into her mouth. 'It's the best anyone can hope for, don't you think? To be remembered. Will you remember me, Roxy?'

'You're not going anywhere?' Roxy was alarmed at the prospect. Already this older girl was her friend. Someone she could truly rely on in a strange new world.

Anne Marie patted her beloved bump. 'Not yet.' She counted her fingers. 'June, July. That's when my baby's due. Then, I'll be gone.'

July. It seemed a lifetime away to Roxy. The whole summer to look forward to first. Then, she'd be here alone, until her own time came. August.

'You'll have made more friends before that, Roxy.' Anne Marie put an arm around her shoulders. 'New girls arrive all the time.'

But not like Anne Marie, she was sure. She could never be this friendly with the loud and common Babs, or with Agnes, with the secret past and the horsey face. She would never trust any of them, or any of the other girls for that matter. Anne Marie was different, exactly what a big sister ought to be – someone to depend on and to talk to – and if the thought popped into Roxy's head that she had never been that kind of big sister to Jennifer, she quickly pushed it out again.

Anyway, Roxy thought, as another troublesome notion hit her, all the new girls seemed to be foreign – Asian or East European with no understanding of English. How was she to make friends with them?

Anne Marie squeezed closer to her on the bench. She looked all around her to check that no one was listening before she whispered, 'I'm going to ask Mrs Dyce if I can come back here to work after my baby's born. They don't even have to pay me. Bed and board, for me and Aidan. I'll be able to do more cleaning and help to look after the girls. I'd be happy to stay here, Roxy. This is the happiest I've ever been in my life.'

No wonder she loved Mrs Dyce like a mother. No wonder she had no qualms about the rules and regulations that seemed so suspicious to Roxy. No wonder she defended everything they did here. Anne Marie had never lived with this kind of security.

'I think that would be a great idea,' Roxy said. 'But they don't like babies here. You said so. What would you do about Aidan?'

'I haven't quite figured that out yet. But I'll come up with something. Because I could never be parted from him.'

Three weeks later and Agnes was gone. She'd gone into labour in the middle of the night and woke the whole house with her screaming.

'Is it really that bad, having a baby?' Roxy asked Anne Marie as she stood at the door of their room watching down the corridor, listening to the sounds of yelling and moaning coming from Agnes's room.

'She's the drama queen, that Agnes. Just ignore her. She'll be fine.' Anne Marie pulled Roxy back into the room and closed the door. Roxy had just enough time to see Mrs Dyce steer Agnes towards the delivery room, towards that door marked PRIVATE.

'And that's the last we'll see of Agnes,' she said.

'Probably better that way. Anyway, Agnes is having her baby adopted.'

Roxy climbed back into bed, kicking the covers to the bottom. It was a hot night, too hot to sleep. 'Maybe if you have your baby adopted, Mrs Dyce would let you stay on here.'

Mrs Dyce's answer to Anne Marie's request to stay on had been a reluctant 'no', because of little Aidan, she had said. They simply couldn't have a baby here. But Anne Marie hadn't quite given up yet.

'I couldn't give up my baby, Roxy. He's a part of me already. My soul. My little Aidan. But I'm working on Mrs Dyce. I think I could coax her into anything.' She looked at Roxy for a long time. 'What about you, Roxy, have you decided yet what you're going to do?'

Roxy had changed her mind so often. She would keep the baby. She would give it up. She didn't know what to do. If she'd been going home she would have kept the baby, even if it was just to show them she could fend for herself. But she wasn't sure whether she would go home. After all, she'd taken care of herself pretty well up to now. She shrugged her answer to Anne Marie. The baby didn't seem real to her yet, even though she had her own little bump now. She still couldn't think of him or her as a person whose future she had to consider.

Mrs Dyce told them next morning that Agnes had been 'safely delivered of a little boy'.

It sounded like an announcement from a newspaper to Roxy. Proclaiming a royal birth. 'Can't we see her … and the baby?' Roxy wanted to know.

'They've both gone already,' Mrs Dyce said. Roxy noticed she didn't even look at her.

'I don't see why Agnes couldn't have come back. She wasn't keeping the baby anyway.' Roxy knew she sounded annoyed, but she didn't care. She wanted an answer. 'What's the point of sending her away?'

Roxy was sure she could see a flash of anger in Mrs Dyce's eyes. But it passed so quickly she couldn't be sure.

It was Anne Marie who jumped in with an answer. 'Sure they can't make any exceptions, Roxy. Isn't that right, Mrs Dyce?'

Mrs Dyce's benign smile was there again, for Anne Marie. Maybe it's just me she doesn't like, Roxy was thinking. I seem to have that effect on people. Roxy almost smiled at the thought. It pleased her to be a thorn in anyone's flesh.

'Unfortunately, that is the case. We've tried it other ways, Roxy, and there's always one of the girls who's disturbed or affected.' Mrs Dyce made to leave the room, but Roxy hadn't finished yet.

'Can't we just see a picture of the baby?' Roxy watched Mrs Dyce's back straighten and she turned slowly, the smile still in place.

'I'll see what I can do,' she said, and then she left them.

But they never did see a photograph of Agnes's baby. Mrs Dyce never mentioned it again and none of the other girls asked. So, finally, neither did Roxy. But it bothered her, like so many things here.

Yet she had only been treated with kindness and concern. That was the thought that kept intruding. Why was she so suspicious? She was worrying herself for nothing. Always looking for a dark side of human nature. She decided to forget about it and just enjoy the summer.

The temperature soared as June moved into a sweltering July and Anne Marie grew too big and heavy to walk with Roxy, so Roxy took to wandering and exploring by herself. She loved the smells of the countryside, trying to pick out the different scents that came from each flower. Not a day now went by when she didn't think about her mother. What was she doing this hot summer? Worrying about her? Or had she forgotten her wayward daughter already?

When she had walked with Anne Marie they had always stayed on the well-worn paths, but that was never Roxy's way. 'If there's a sign that says NO TRESPASSING, that's where Roxy will go,' her dad had always said to her, with pride. Yet that was the part of her personality that only ever seemed to annoy her mother. And worry her too. The part that would do what she wasn't supposed to.

Now, here she was, pushing her way through the long grass, thick and rich and crackling dry with summer, and heading towards the wrought-iron gates that lay at the bottom of the long drive. The gates that kept the world out, and kept the girls in. She didn't use the main path because she didn't want anyone, the Dyces, or even Stevens, to see where she was going, afraid they would stop her, suspect her of disobeying the rule and straying outside. The gates were ornate and from a distance it was hard to make out what the design of them was. It was only as she came closer that she could make out what the swirls and curls were.

Dragons. Dragons rampant and threatening, wrought-iron fire shooting from their nostrils.

The rusted gates were chained closed. And Roxy didn't like that at all. Mrs Dyce had asked her not to go outside, but she hadn't mentioned anything about being locked in.

Roxy suddenly wanted desperately to get out. Normally, she would have climbed the gates. Even now, she was looking for footholds in the curls and swirls that were dragons' tails and claws and tongues of fire. Dragons.

They were everywhere.

Here be dragons.

Wasn't that a warning of some kind?

She grasped the gate with both hands. Even in the

sweltering heat, the iron was cold to the touch as she clasped her hands round a dragon's tail. Of course, she couldn't climb. Not now. Not with this bump.

She hated that bump at that moment. Resented it. Because of that bump, she couldn't leave here. She was trapped. Locked gates, rusty with age, and high grass, and unkempt grounds apart from the drive and right in front of the house. Why?

And one odd-job man to help.

Suspicions rose in her again. There was a mystery here, she was sure of it.

She stood for what seemed an age, just gazing outside.

'You don't want to go climbing there.' The harsh voice made her jump and she turned in alarm.

It was Stevens. His face was tanned like worn brown leather, his hair as wild as the grass around them, and he had a stubble of a beard. But it was his hands her eyes were drawn to, his fingers tightly clasping a shovel, those maggot-like fingers. She imagined them around her throat, squeezing.

She began to sweat.

'I wasn't going to climb,' she said quickly.

'You shouldn't even be here.' His voice was like sandpaper.

She began to try to explain that she'd got lost, was looking for the way back, any lie, until she realised he didn't mean here, beside the gates. He meant she shouldn't be at this Dragon House at all. Dragon House, it was the first time she had thought of it like that.

'You're too young,' he rasped. 'I told them you were too young. You should be home with your mother.'

He took a step towards her and Roxy backed herself against the railings.

'One bit of advice I give you. Go home, before it's too late.' It was a husky whisper.

Roxy began to panic. There's no one here, she thought. I'm all alone with this crazy man. Why had she ever come here? Why did she always have to break the rules? He came even closer, so close she could feel his breath on her face. She couldn't stop watching his fingers clench and unclench angrily around the handle of the shovel. Why was he angry? What had she ever done to him?

'What do you mean … before it's too late?'

'You're stupid,' he said. 'You're all stupid. You just get what you deserve.'

'Why?' she snapped, her fear making her angry.

'What are you going on about? They're taking care of us here, aren't they?'

He grinned at her. His teeth, what was left of them, yellow and sharp, like fangs. 'Oh, they're taking care of you all right.'

'What do you mean by that? Tell me!'

'Go home. I'm telling you. That's all I'm going to say. More than my life's worth to say even that.'

More than his life's worth. Hadn't he said that before, to Babs?

'Before it's too late!' She asked him again, 'What does that mean? Too late for what?'

He looked worried now, glancing around him as if someone might jump out of the trees. 'Said too much, said too much. Shut up … shut up.'

He was weird. No, worse than weird, he was scary. And he hated her, she was sure of that.

And she was alone here with him.

CHAPTER THIRTEEN

Roxy made a sudden rush at him, taking him by surprise. She pushed her palms against his chest with all her strength. He stumbled, almost fell, just giving her enough time to dodge round him, and shoot out of his way. She began to run, breathing hard, afraid. Angry too. Why did the Dyces have this weirdo working for them? The last person who should be here among young vulnerable girls. He looked like some deranged homicidal maniac, a pervert. She was going to run straight to the Dyces, tell them to get rid of him, tell them just how scary he was. She glanced behind her, sure she would see him, reaching out for her, closing in on her.

It was the worst thing she could have done. She lost her balance, tried to find something to grasp to keep herself steady, but there was only the long grass, the wild flowers. Roxy fell badly, and hurt her back. She tried not to scream. She tried not to breathe. She let out a low moan and just lay there, hoping he would have moved off, thinking she had gone. She bit her lip and listened. She could hear a swishing through the tall grass. Footsteps striding towards her. He was coming, reaching out for her with those fingers, those nightmare fingers. Every instinct she had told her to get up and run, but she couldn't move. She was too clumsy with this stupid bump holding her back and once again she resented it.

Any moment now, he would be here above her. Any moment now …

'What on earth are you doing down there, my girl?'

It wasn't Stevens. It was Mr Dyce, with his Santa Claus smile. He reached down and gripped her hand to help her up.

'Did you fall, dear? Are you hurt? Do you need to see the doctor?' He fussed about her like an old granny, dusting her down, feeling her brow. 'What happened to you?'

Roxy found her voice. 'It was that weirdo, Stevens. He scared me.'

'Did he say anything? Do anything?'

She steadied herself, thinking how to answer. A

second ago she had thought to tell the Dyces everything Stevens had said, ask them what he meant. 'They're taking care of you all right.' In the moment it took her to answer, something held her back. Some instinct she couldn't explain.

'He's just scary,' she repeated. 'Why have you got someone like that working here? He's weird.'

'He's always worked here, even before we came. He is a good worker.'

'Why can't I get out of the gates? Why are they locked?' Roxy's questions took him by surprise.

'Was that what you were trying to do?'

'I don't see any reason why I can't go outside for a walk, or go to the village. There must be a village nearby.'

He looked flustered. He was never the one who was asked difficult questions. It was always his wife, she was the one always ready with a glib answer.

'It's for your own safety, Roxy. You must understand that. If you go into the village, people might see you, recognise you.'

'Recognise me?' The idea surprised her. 'Why should anyone recognise me? Have I been on the telly? Has my photo been in the papers?' She had a vision of her mother once again, sitting at a table at one of those press conferences, in a tearful appeal begging her daughter to come home.

Sweat was breaking out on his forehead. Was he so nervous? Or was it the heat? It was such a hot afternoon perhaps that could explain it.

'Maybe at the beginning, there was some publicity. But the police soon lose interest when it's clear that a young person has run away, and doesn't want to be found.' He took Roxy by the elbow and led her back to the house. 'It's not as if you've been kidnapped or anything.' He giggled as if he'd made a very funny joke.

Not kidnapped. No. But she wasn't allowed out, was she? The gates were locked, and she was kept inside.

'But just a walk outside, what would be the harm in that?'

'Plenty of places to go walking inside the grounds, dear,' he said, and in truth that seemed a perfectly logical answer.

As were all of their answers, all of their explanations. All perfectly logical. She seemed to be the only one to question everything. Roxy remembered Sula who'd gone home to her family, and she felt guilty. The Dyces had helped Sula get home. They had only ever helped her. She walked back to the house with Mr Dyce while he prattled on, gossiping like an old maid. He was a nice old man. She too could go home whenever she wanted, she told herself, and they would help her. They had only ever helped her, the Dyces. She tried to think like Anne Marie, but all the time there was a feeling as if something heavy was lying in her heart. Maybe it was guilt, she told herself over and over. Guilt about how much she distrusted the Dyces, and guilt about what she had done to her mother.

She would write to her.

The decision came in a flash. She would tell her mother that she was safe and well, and that there was no need to come looking for her. She would promise to get in touch again, soon. Roxy didn't want her worrying, or crying on television over her.

Although, deep down, there was also a fear that her mother wasn't worrying or crying. That, with Paul and Jennifer there beside her, Roxy, her wayward daughter, had been quickly forgotten.

A few days later, on a sultry afternoon, Babs went into labour. Roxy couldn't believe how calm she was as she packed up her bag and got ready to leave them. Wasn't she nervous?

'Know what's coming,' she answered her, casually. 'This isn't my first, you know.'

Roxy was shocked. She hadn't realised that at all. Babs, for all her worldliness, was only a young girl. 'You've had a baby before?'

Babs nodded.

'Where is it?'

'Had it adopted.' She said it as if it didn't matter. 'Or I should say, the Dyces got somebody to take it.'

'The Dyces? You've been here before?'

'That's why I knew to come this time. The last time they picked me up, just the way they did you, and they took me here. When the sprog was born, they sorted everything. Gave me money, good bit of money.' She raised her eyebrows with glee at the thought of that money. 'So, naturally, I came back here again. Wasn't going to pass this up, was I?'

Roxy looked at Babs as if for the first time. She realised she didn't like her. Babs was funny and common and loud – but she was selfish and heartless too.

'You'll get money this time too?'

Babs knew by Roxy's tone how she felt about that. Her face grew hard. 'So what? I thought you were getting yours adopted too. You'll get money. You're not any better than I am.'

Roxy didn't know how to answer that. Selfish and heartless, was that her too?

A flash of pain crossed Babs's face. 'Mrs Dyce!' she screamed. 'Time I was going.'

Mrs Dyce came hurrying in and took her by the arm. 'Come along, Babs.'

Babs waved cheerily to everyone as she waddled off. Roxy was the only one who didn't wave back. She just stood trying to take in what Babs had just told her. Now she was sure she knew what was happening here.

They were selling their babies.

CHAPTER FOURTEEN

'Of course they're not selling our babies! Roxy, what a thing to say!' Anne Marie was more amused than shocked when she told her what she thought.

'You can't see anything bad in anything they do, Anne Marie. But there's something fishy going on here.'

It was their turn to make the evening meal, along with one of the new girls, dark-skinned, silent, with hardly any English. She looked perpetually frightened. She was already heavily pregnant and would undoubtedly drop her baby before Anne Marie. She sat at the big table in the middle of the kitchen peeling potatoes. When Anne Marie laughed, she looked round at her, but didn't smile.

Anne Marie had a musical laugh, almost like a tune. It made Roxy smile, even though she was trying hard to be serious.

'Fishy. How appropriate, we're having fish for tea. Salmon cakes.'

Roxy wouldn't let it go. 'Babs told me they gave her money the last time. They're giving her money this time too. Anne Marie, they're buying our babies and selling them for adoption.'

Anne Marie stopped what she was doing and looked at Roxy very seriously. 'You listened to Babs? Babs is what your mother would call a "loose woman", any looser and she would fall apart.' Then she laughed again. 'Mind, my mother would have a cheek calling any woman loose. However, Babs is the type who *would* sell her baby, to the highest bidder too. But the Dyces would only have given her money to try to help her get started again. The money was to help her, not to buy her baby.'

'So, where did the baby go? Who adopted it? When people want to adopt a baby they have to go through checks. Rigorous checks. The authorities have to make sure they're the right kind of people, decent people.'

'The Dyces do make sure they're letting decent people adopt the babies. I'm sure of it. I trust them.'

But then, Anne Marie trusted everything about the

Dyces, didn't she? thought Roxy.

'Anyway,' she went on, 'I'm not having my baby adopted. I'm keeping Aidan.'

That was the moment Roxy made up her mind. She was keeping hers too. It was also at that moment she realised her baby was no longer 'the bump'. It had become her baby.

And no one was going to sell her baby.

After dinner all the girls sat outside in the evening sun. Too hot to stay indoors and even uncomfortably hot outside. Summer smells scented the air. Roxy and Anne Marie lay on the grass and watched the first star appear in the blue sky. One by one the other girls drifted inside the house, but not them. It was too beautiful.

Roxy watched as the moon cast silver lights on the roof of the house, on the attic windows. 'I wonder how you get into the rest of the house,' she said, almost to herself.

'I think that would be through the Dyces' apartments, probably.'

Roxy wasn't so sure. 'You think so? I mean, there must be a staircase up to the next floors, there must be some kind of corridor leading into the rest of the house. I think it's strange we've never actually seen it. It's as if, if we stepped into that other part of the house we would be in a different world.'

'Aren't you the one with the imagination, Roxy.' Anne Marie laughed. But a thought had been planted in Roxy's mind. She was going to find the entrance to those attics, and do a bit of exploring. If she couldn't wander outside the grounds, then nothing was going to stop her wandering inside.

Anne Marie breathed in deeply. 'It's nights like this that make life worth living,' she said softly.

Roxy leaned up on her elbow and watched her as she studied the sky dreamily. 'For someone who's had such a hard life you always look on the bright side of every-thing, don't you?'

'And for someone who's always had it so cushy, you are the most cynical person I have ever come across.'

'Cushy? You think I've had it cushy?'

'Yes, I do. A mum and dad who loved you, a little sis-ter you … used … to get on with. A home. Yes. I think you've had it cushy.'

'Until my dad died. Then everything changed.'

Anne Marie struggled to sit up. Roxy had to help her.

She stared at Roxy. 'Maybe it was you who changed. Your dad died, but Jennifer's dad died too, and she didn't go off the rails. Your mum's husband died, and she didn't go wild.'

'She got married again,' Roxy reminded her.

'So, she got married again. I bet your dad would have wanted that for her.'

'Whose side are you on?'

Anne Marie smiled. 'It's not a case of sides, but from what you tell me, I think you should take your baby home. I think your mum would welcome you with open arms.'

Roxy dismissed that suggestion. 'I'm never going home. I've done all right by myself up till now. I'll do just as well when my baby comes.'

'Your baby?' Anne Marie grabbed her into a hug. 'That's the first time you've called him "your baby".'

She was still hugging her when Mrs Dyce turned the corner of the house and approached them. She seemed startled to find them there, still sitting in the twilight. 'I thought all you girls had gone to bed.'

Anne Marie got to her feet and brushed the grass from her trousers. 'It's such a beautiful night, we didn't want to waste it.'

Mrs Dyce turned her face to the sky. 'Yes, it is, isn't it?'

'How's Babs?' Roxy asked, and there it was again, that tight smile. Surely she couldn't be mistaken about that.

'Babs is doing fine. She had a little girl.'

Anne Marie clapped her hands together enthusiastically. 'Oh, that is so lovely.'

'Can we see her? Is she still here?' asked Roxy.

'Babs is gone already.'

'How did she go? In an ambulance? We never see any ambulances coming or going. So, how do the girls leave, and the babies?' Roxy was asking too many questions. She could read that in Mrs Dyce's eyes.

'Young girls are usually fit enough to leave in a car, Roxy. The delivery room has its own exit, that's why you don't see them going. We make sure the girls are well wrapped up, and rested before they leave. As for the babies who are being adopted, they're in tiny bassinets. We put them safely in the back seat and take them to their new families. Does that answer all your questions now?'

'You don't waste any time, do you?'

Mrs Dyce didn't even look at Roxy when she said that. But she did look when Roxy asked the next question.

'Can we see the baby? After all, Babs won't have taken the baby with her. Is her baby still here?'

It was as if her smile was fixed to her face. She never got a chance to think up an answer, if that's what she was intending to do. Anne Marie burst in with her happy laugh. 'You'll never guess what suspicious little Roxy thinks is happening here. She only thinks you're selling babies.'

There was no mistaking the shock on Mrs Dyce's face this time. Her head swivelled round so fast Roxy thought it was going to be like that scene from *The Exorcist*.

'What on earth gave you such an idea?'

'Babs,' Anne Marie answered for Roxy. 'Babs told her she'd been here before and you gave her money.'

The tension seemed to ooze out of Mrs Dyce. Her thin shoulders dropped and she breathed out slowly. A sigh of relief. That's how it seemed to Roxy.

'We gave her money to help her start a new life. We never expected to see her again. And then, when she was brought back to us in the same condition ... what could we do but help her again?'

Anne Marie punched Roxy's shoulder. 'There. What did I tell you?'

'But who adopts the babies? How do you know they're decent respectable people?'

Mrs Dyce pushed her balled fists deep into the pockets of her cardigan. 'Don't you think we run checks on everyone? Probably more thorough checks than any of the social services. We, after all, don't have to be politically correct. If we don't think a couple are suitable we don't have to make excuses.' She wasn't smiling now. She was holding something in check. Anger at Roxy and her nosiness probably. 'There are so many people out there who just aren't eligible with the proper authorities, older couples for instance. And even after the adoption has gone through we keep a check on them to make sure the babies are doing well, being treated well. Does that satisfy you, Roxy?'

Roxy only said, 'Is it legal?'

Anne Marie took a step closer to Mrs Dyce. Her face seemed to say that Roxy was asking too many questions. But Roxy wasn't ready to stop now.

'It just doesn't sound as if the law knows about these babies, or these couples. How do they explain where they get their babies from?'

She could hear frogs from the stream close by, croaking in the hot summer night. Otherwise there wasn't a sound.

Mrs Dyce took her hands from her pockets and waved them around, at the house, at the grounds. 'All this isn't legal, Roxy. Legally, we should be handing you over to the authorities. We should hand over a lot of the girls, the illegal immigrants especially. I can't do that to them. I want to help … you … and them. So, I keep you here, illegally. You can go any time you want, I have told you that before. All I ask is a promise not to tell anyone about this place. If I'm doing a wicked thing, then that's too bad. I think I'm helping girls. Girls like you, Roxy.' She wasn't hiding her annoyance this time.

Anne Marie put an arm around the woman's shoulders. 'You are, Mrs Dyce. Roxy doesn't mean what she said, she's just curious.'

Mrs Dyce patted Anne Marie's arm. 'I'll say goodnight, girls. Don't stay up too long.' Only then did she look at Roxy. 'You can be quite hurtful at times, Roxy.'

Roxy and Anne Marie didn't say a word as they watched her disappear round the house. Then Anne Marie turned on Roxy. 'You've hurt her feelings, Roxy.

127

You're always questioning everything. I think you should apologise to her.'

But there was no way Roxy was going to apologise to Mrs Dyce. Not until she found out exactly what was happening here.

CHAPTER FIFTEEN

Anne Marie wouldn't let it go. It worried her that Roxy had offended her beloved Mrs Dyce. 'Where would you be without the Dyces, and have they ever shown you anything but kindness?'

In the end, she talked Roxy into apologising. Maybe Mrs Dyce *was* 'selling' babies, but if she was helping girls like herself – even girls like Babs – and if they were helping couples to have the children they were desperate for and, most important of all, settling a baby in a loving home, then who was Roxy to complain? It was the thought of how Babs would bring up a baby that helped her change her mind. Babs's baby was much better off being adopted.

But Mrs Dyce wasn't getting Roxy's. Roxy knew that now. No one was.

Roxy's baby.

How was it that now it filled her heart just thinking

about that baby, growing inside her, with tiny feet and fingers? Curled up in the safest place in the world.

Inside Roxy.

Roxy could look after herself. She had proved that. And when she had some tiny little someone else depending on her, she would look after them both.

As soon as she told Anne Marie about her decision, she insisted that Roxy apologise to Mrs Dyce the very next day. 'Sure you've hurt her feelings. And, fair play to her, Roxy, she did tell you the truth. She is having some of the babies adopted. What she's doing here is illegal, she admits that. We're the ones with the power. We could tell on her any time.'

That was what swayed Roxy in the end. Mrs Dyce had admitted everything. Surely, she thought, there couldn't be anything else to tell.

Yet it seemed that just as one question was answered, another would surface.

Roxy watched for Mrs Dyce from the kitchen, saw her driving up in the old jeep and pulling to a halt. She had obviously been for provisions. (So somewhere nearby, Roxy thought, there had to be a village.) She waited until Mrs Dyce started unloading the boxes of fruit and vegetables from the jeep before she hurried outside to help her.

Mrs Dyce waved her aside. 'No, no, Roxy. You can't carry anything heavy.'

'It's only a couple of cauliflowers. They're not going to do me much damage,' Roxy said. Neither of them looked the other in the eye.

As they were putting the shopping away in the kitchen, Roxy said, 'Can I speak to you?'

Mrs Dyce turned to look at her and seemed to suck in her cheeks. 'What is it now, Roxy?' Her husky voice sounded just on the edge of anger.

'I want to apologise,' Roxy said at once. She didn't want the woman to be angry with her. Because what if they decided to put her out, expel her like Eve from the Garden of Eden. Where would she go? What would she do?

However, as soon as Roxy spoke the coldness in Mrs Dyce's eyes melted away.

Roxy hurried on. 'I know I ask too many questions. I won't ask any more.'

Mrs Dyce shook her head and smiled. 'Yes, you will, Roxy. I don't think you'll ever stop asking questions.'

'I wanted you to know that I am grateful you took me

in. I really am. I don't know where I would be without you.'

Mrs Dyce pulled her close and hugged her. Now, *that*, Roxy didn't like. It smacked too much of an American sitcom.

'You've said enough, Roxy. Let's just forget it, shall we?'

Roxy was so happy to be back in Mrs Dyce's good books she almost felt like crying. It was so silly to feel like that, she told herself, yet she couldn't help it. She only hoped her next request wasn't going to spoil things again.

'Can I send a letter to my mother?'

'Do you want to go home?' She couldn't read Mrs Dyce's face at that point. She had turned towards the cupboard and was stacking tins inside.

Home was the last place Roxy wanted to be at the moment. 'I just want her to know I'm all right. I won't tell her about the baby.' It occurred then to Roxy that what Mrs Dyce would fear most would be Roxy telling her mother about the set-up here. She wanted to reassure her about that. 'I'm not going to tell her where I am. You can read the letter when I've written it.'

Mrs Dyce's shoulders visibly relaxed. 'No need for

that. Of course you must write your letter. I'll see it's posted. I think it's an excellent idea.'

And if she really wanted Roxy to write to her mother, then why should Roxy ever be suspicious again? She promised herself she never would be. Like Anne Marie she would accept everything here, and be grateful.

Roxy started that letter a dozen times, then crumpled up the paper and hurled it in the bin. In the end what she wrote could have fitted on a postcard. 'I'm safe and well. Don't look for me. I'll write again soon. Roxy.'

No 'love'. Not even a 'Dear Mum'. Terms of affection she couldn't bring herself to use. Maybe her mother didn't love her any more after what she'd done. Maybe none of them wanted to hear from her ever again.

It was almost a week before she gave the letter to Mrs Dyce, one night after dinner. Mrs Dyce took it and slipped it in her pocket. 'I'll have it posted tomorrow, Roxy.' She said it brightly, as if they were friends again.

'You won't be posting it from anywhere near here, will you?' Roxy couldn't help notice the hesitation in Mrs Dyce's eyes. 'You can tell me the truth, I understand. If the letter is posted from here, my mother might just come to this area looking for me … I wouldn't want that. Neither would you. Of course you have to post it from somewhere else.'

Mrs Dyce stared at her. 'You really are something else, Roxy. You should be a detective. You're quite right. I'll have someone post it from London. It wouldn't just be you who would be in danger if the postmark was local. It would be all these girls here.'

Roxy looked around her. All these girls here were now mostly dark-skinned, frightened and alone. Illegal immigrants, dumped when they were pregnant. No English. There was only herself and Anne Marie left of the original crowd. No more nights piled into each other's rooms, like boarding school. No more midnight feasts. Everyone kept to themselves. Everything was changing here, Roxy thought.

She felt better after she had given Mrs Dyce that letter. At least she had let them know she was safe. That she wasn't dead, that she hadn't been murdered or kidnapped. That she was alive and well.

That night as they lay in bed she asked Anne Marie if she had ever thought of writing home.

'Me? You've got to be joking. I wouldn't risk them finding out where I was and coming after me. Not to look after me, mind, just to thump the living daylights out of me. Do you know something, Roxy? Mr and Mrs Dyce, they're my family now. And you too. You're like my little sister.'

Suddenly, a wonderfully bright idea hit Roxy like a thunderbolt. She jumped up in bed. 'Anne Marie, why don't we live together after the babies are born? We could help each other, and we do get on really well.'

But Anne Marie didn't sound too certain. 'Sure, that would be a great idea, but you're under age Roxy, it isn't going to be so easy for you.'

Roxy knew that was going to be a big problem, one she wasn't ready to face right now. But the thought of sharing the future with Anne Marie suddenly seemed so right.

She sat on Anne Marie's bed. 'I'm sure the Dyces would sort things out for us. Find somewhere for us to live, maybe. They would keep in touch. You could still see them.'

Anne Marie smiled. 'Do you know, Roxy, this might be the perfect answer. You and me, and our babies, all together.'

They lay back in their beds giggling and talking about the future. The bedroom window was wide open to let in some air, and the sky was clear with bright stars. It seemed to both of them that night that nothing could go wrong.

Anne Marie's face, with her apple-red cheeks, beamed happily in the moonlight. 'Roxy, do you know, I think our story's going to have a happy ending.'

CHAPTER SIXTEEN

Mrs Dyce liked the girls to rest in the afternoon, insisting they pull down the shades to darken the rooms, and keep out the hot sun.

Anne Marie loved her afternoon rest, especially now, so near her time. But not Roxy. She could never sleep and she hated lying on her bed, listening to the gentle snores of the other girls drifting in through the open doors. But the house was never so quiet as on those afternoons, and Roxy used the time exploring. She was determined to find a way into those attics, into those other rooms, blocked off from the rest of the house.

She had already found stairs that led nowhere, that seemed to disappear into walls, and doors that were locked, or even boarded up, but on one of her hot afternoon explorations she found exactly what she had been looking for.

She had often walked past the back stairs.

Underneath was stacked with old carpets and bags of clothes and boxes and chairs. Up against the back wall there was an upended table. Just a load of old rubbish, she had always thought as she walked past it. But that day, something made her stop and look more closely. It occurred to her that the back wall had to lead on to the back of the house. She moved closer into the gloom, lifting boxes, moving carpets as silently as she could, trying to clear a way to the back, to the upended table that blocked the back wall. But close up she realised the table would be far too heavy for her to move on her own. Still, she refused to give up. Could she get behind it? she wondered. It wasn't flush against the wall, but stood at an angle, and as she crept closer she could see behind that gap. She could see that there was a door behind the table.

She knew she had to get through to that door. Nothing was going to stop her now. If she had to pick the lock, if she had to break the door down, she was determined to do it. That door had to lead into the rest of the house.

It would be tight, she knew that. But she was carrying this bump of hers neatly, everyone said that. 'You'd hardly know you were pregnant,' Anne Marie would tell her. Roxy stretched out her hand between the gap to grasp the door handle, half expecting it to refuse to turn, to be locked. But it wasn't. She gasped as the door opened, and with a quick look back to make sure she hadn't been seen, Roxy squeezed behind the table and stepped through the door.

She found herself in a dark, musty corridor. At the far end a narrow window was shuttered closed, but through the gaps in the shutters streams of light shone through. The bottom half of the walls was panelled with dark wood, the top half had ancient paper peeling from it. She stepped gingerly along the hallway, hardly daring to breathe. There was a smell in here, the smell of long-dead rooms. At the end of the corridor was a door leading to narrow winding staircase and she began to climb. These would have been the servants' quarters long ago. She was sure of that. No lady would ever have been allowed to use a tiny cramped staircase like this. There would have been no room for their ornate dresses, for a start.

There was a door at the top of the stairs too, and this one creaked open so noisily that it made Roxy catch her breath, afraid someone might hear. She stood for a moment listening, waiting for a call, or footsteps, but there was nothing. She realised she must be in the main part of the house. She was standing in a hallway that must have once been quite grand. Dusty curtains half hung on high windows. Chairs lay upended on the floor, and thick brocade tapestries rotted against the walls.

She began to walk, warily, stepping as quietly as she could. She opened a door into one of the rooms, but once again there were only shuttered windows and rotting draperies. No one had been inside this part of the house for years. Yet the part the girls lived in was bright and newly painted. It reminded her of something. She had to think for a moment of what that something was. Then it hit her. It was as if the front of the house, where the girls lived, was the stage in a theatre. Brightly lit, furnished, with actors playing their parts. Here was the back of the theatre, dull, unused and dusty. And it was cold. Though the sun scorched the earth outside it was as if Nature had turned off her heating in these rooms.

There was a mystery here, there had to be. 'Aren't you the one with the imagination,' Anne Marie would say. But there was a mystery here. Why was one part of the house so bright, taken care of, and another, this part, just left to fall apart? She could hear Anne Marie's glib answer to that. 'It's expensive enough for them to heat and run this part, you can't expect them to open the whole house up just for us.'

But this was their house – the Dyces had said so. And this part wasn't just closed up, with white sheets covering furniture, as if it was waiting for someone to claim it again. This part of the house had been long forgotten. It looked as if it should be condemned.

Condemned. She didn't like the sound of that.

Here too, carved into doors, on fireplaces, even on the ancient wallpaper, dragons were everywhere. This was indeed Dragon House.

Roxy climbed another flight of stairs and found herself on the attic floor. Here she found a warren of small rooms, musty and empty, except for rubbish stacked against walls or on the floor. There were more broken chairs, moth-eaten carpets, old curtains. One room had obviously once been a nursery. She found a library too. One room still stacked high with books. Roxy lifted one from a shelf and opened it. Dust exploded from it, the pages almost fell apart. She dropped it to the floor and sent dust leaping all around the dark room. Roxy began to sneeze, tried to stop herself and couldn't. She held her shirt against her nose and looked around. In the middle of the library there was a spiral staircase leading to a landing above. Once, long ago, this must have been a favourite spot for relaxing. A place to come with a book, climb the staircase, sit by the top window and look out at the view.

The view. She saw that through the one small window on that landing a strip of light was shining through the shutters. What might she see from there?

The spiral staircase was rickety and shook with every step she took, but it was worth the journey. From the landing window she could see below her a pathway that led from the Dyces' apartments, from that room marked PRIVATE; a pathway which led to the delivery room, a square, brick building separate from the main house. She could see the exit door from here too. The door Mrs Dyce had told her about. The door through which everyone must leave, here, at the back of the house, secluded and sealed off. No wonder no one was ever seen leaving. Roxy sat there for a long time. Now she knew how the girls and their babies left Dragon House. They went through the Dyces' apartments, down the path and into the delivery room, and then one by one, they all left, silently, secretly, from here.

She didn't know how long she sat there, thinking and watching. But when she finally checked her watch she knew she had to hurry. She didn't want anyone to know she had found this secret place. She would tell Anne Marie, but only her, and swear her to secrecy.

Roxy was covered in dust and cobwebs when she came down towards the bottom corridor again. She stopped to dust herself down before going back through the door under the stairs, when she heard voices coming through the wall. She realised she was listening to the Dyces in their private office. There was no way she wasn't going to listen to this. She had to strain her ears to hear them, only catching snatches of what they were saying.

'More girls,' Mr Dyce was saying. 'Is that wise?'

And his wife's answer. 'More girls,' and her voice was so husky Roxy only just caught her last words, 'economically viable'.

'Economically viable'? What did that mean?

Two new girls arrived next day. (The 'more girls' Mr Dyce had been referring to, Roxy wondered?) Both of them foreign. One was Asian and rejected any attempt at friendliness. But the other was a wary, silent black girl, Aneeka. She was an illegal immigrant. They all knew that without asking. She trusted no one and ate in a corner by herself.

Anne Marie was the one who tried to be friendly, squeezing up beside her, miming conversation because Aneeka spoke no English. It was no use. She turned away, her dark eyes wide with fear, afraid to trust anyone.

'I don't understand how they found her,' Roxy said to Anne Marie. 'She can't speak any English, so she couldn't have told anyone she needed help.' Yet she had found her way to the Dyces.

Anne Marie had a ready answer. 'They have contacts everywhere. Word of mouth.' She stared at Roxy long and hard. 'Don't tell me you're still suspicious?'

She knew that Roxy was. Roxy had told the older girl about her expedition, making her promise to keep the secret. Anne Marie had warned her that it could have been dangerous, she could have been trapped there and no one would have known where she was. Sensible stuff. Even when Roxy had told her about the Dyces' conversation she had another ready answer. '"Economically viable." Well, if they brought more girls they might feel they would have to open more of the house, and it would take too much money to decorate it and make it liveable in. They probably mean that using the whole house *wouldn't* be economically viable. It would be too expensive to run. You didn't hear all they were saying, Roxy.'

So Roxy shrugged her shoulders and decided not to make too much of it. But new girls, foreign girls, how could they be more 'economically viable'? Unless, the more babies they sell, the more money they made. Because they *were* selling the babies, no matter what Mrs Dyce said, no matter what Anne Marie believed. That was the answer for Roxy and she didn't like it.

Aneeka wasn't with them for long.

One hot night, two days after Aneeka had arrived, Roxy was awakened by her sobbing. It was hard to sleep it was so hot, and the windows and doors were all opened wide to let in some air, and when she got up out of bed there was Aneeka, crouched in the corridor, her arms wrapped round her legs, her face buried in her knees.

'Aneeka OK?' Roxy knelt beside her with difficulty. She held up her thumb in an international gesture. Aneeka only looked at her and her eyes flashed with fear.

'It's me … Roxy' she said softly, smiling. Aneeka's face was streaked with tears. She didn't smile back, she just stared. Roxy kept smiling, not knowing what else to do. Feeling like an idiot.

Suddenly, Aneeka bared her teeth like a wild animal and she started shouting. She gave Roxy such a fright she fell backwards. At that, Aneeka leaned over her, grabbed her by the shoulders and started shaking her. Now, Roxy was terrified.

'Anne Marie!' she shouted.

By now, Aneeka was almost hysterical. She wouldn't let Roxy go. She was crying and yelling and all at once the corridor was filled with girls waddling from their rooms, pulling on dressing gowns. They all started shouting.

'Doesn't anyone speak her language?' Roxy yelled. 'What's she saying?'

Anne Marie tried to put her arm around Aneeka, but she threw it off angrily. And then she said the only English words Roxy had ever heard her speak, and they frightened the life out of her.

'Kill baby!' And she jabbed at her stomach. 'Kill baby!'

She bent over Roxy, and grabbed her face in her hands. 'Kill baby! Kill baby!' Over and over again she said it, and she was still saying it when Mrs Dyce appeared, running towards them. She was shouting Aneeka's name, trying to drown out her words.

She dropped down beside them and hugged Aneeka close. Aneeka seemed even more terrified. She tried to push her away, so violently that she almost sent her sprawling on the ground. But Mrs Dyce still gripped her firmly and lifted her to her feet. 'Come with me, Aneeka. Come, my dear.'

Aneeka was shaking her head, trying not to go. She held on to Roxy's robe and looked into her eyes. Hers were filled with panic and fear. It was as if she wanted Roxy to help her. Something in Roxy wanted to run after her, wanted desperately to keep her here with the rest of the girls.

Finally, she couldn't stop herself. 'She said, "kill baby", Mrs Dyce!' She shouted it up the corridor and there was a hushed silence from everyone. Except Mrs Dyce. She didn't even lose a step, or look back. She waved a hand behind her to quieten her.

'I'll come back later and speak to you, Roxy.' That was all she said, and then she was gone, closing the door marked PRIVATE on a sobbing, terrified Aneeka.

One by one the girls all started drifting back to their

rooms as if nothing had happened.

Roxy couldn't believe it. 'Am I the only one who's worried about that? She said … "kill baby".'

Anne Marie put her arms round her. 'She probably wants rid of it,' she said coldly. 'And she hasn't got enough English to ask politely, "Could I have a termination, please?"' She said it in a very posh accent and Roxy knew she was trying to make her feel better, but it had the opposite effect. It made her angry at her friend. She didn't think there was anything funny about what had happened. She looked at Anne Marie.

'Is that what you think?'

'Frankly, yes I do,' she said. 'But we'll ask Mrs Dyce later.'

'"We'll ask Mrs Dyce later",' Roxy mimicked Anne Marie's Irish brogue. 'And whatever Mrs Dyce tells us, we'll believe.'

'You,' Anne Marie pinched at her cheeks, 'are a little revolutionary! Do you know that?'

How could Roxy explain to anyone, even to herself, that every time she put her suspicions behind her, a new one popped up, like weeds in a garden.

*   *   *

148

She couldn't sleep all that night, thinking about Aneeka, wondering what was happening to her and her baby. Mrs Dyce spoke to Anne Marie and her at breakfast. She came into the kitchen and told them very gravely, 'I'm sorry about last night, girls. That must have been very upsetting for you all. I think Mr Dyce and I made a grave error of judgement in bringing Aneeka here. She was very disturbed. But we wanted to help her so much.' She paused for a moment, as if it was too hard for her to carry on. 'She didn't want this baby. I'm sure you realised that already. It brought great shame on her family. She would never have been able to go home with a baby.'

'So how is she now?' Anne Marie asked softly.

'She's had her wish, I'm afraid. She lost the baby.'

Anne Marie gasped.

'We did everything we could to save her,' Mrs Dyce continued. 'But it was no use.'

'So where is Aneeka now?' There was no softness in Roxy's voice.

'We've sent her on to the next house.'

'Not to hospital? Shouldn't she be in a hospital?'

'Mrs Dyce is a nurse, Roxy. She knows what she's doing.'

For the first time Roxy lost her temper with Anne Marie.

'Honestly, Anne Marie, do you just believe everything?! Aneeka's terrified. She's screaming, "Kill baby!" and now, very conveniently, her baby is dead. OK, I'm willing to believe that, but if she lost the baby, then she must need special treatment. Surely the delivery room here isn't equipped for every emergency.'

Mrs Dyce was annoyed now, tightlipped, but still with a ready answer.

'If anything went badly wrong, Roxy, I can assure you we would have no hesitation in sending both mother and baby to hospital. Do you honestly think, after all we've done for you, that we would risk any of your lives?'

She sounded annoyed again. Even though her voice remained as ever, soft. Maybe she had a reason to be annoyed, Roxy thought.

'Anyway, I have had a very difficult night. I just wanted to let you know about Aneeka. And to apologise.'

Anne Marie was quick to assure her that there was no need for that apology. But not Roxy, and she could see that Mrs Dyce was perfectly aware of that. Roxy felt sick, as if a lump of lead lay inside her along with her baby.

After her chores were done Roxy went back to bed. She couldn't stop thinking about Aneeka. How frightened she'd been last night. And now they'd never see her again. Like the other girls, she had passed through the doors leading to the delivery room, and disappeared. They could have been zapped up by aliens, or been transported into another dimension. The thought scared her.

Anne Marie came in and sat on the bed beside her. 'I wish you'd stop your worrying.' She stroked Roxy's brow with her soft hands.

'I don't want to go into that delivery room alone, Anne Marie,' Roxy said. For it seemed to Roxy that when you went in there you were never seen again.

'Neither do I,' Anne Marie said.

Roxy knew then what they had to do, and it brightened her up right away. 'Me and you will be birth partners. We'll help each other through it, OK?'

Roxy's cousin had had a baby and her birth partner had been her sister. She remembered that now. Remembered how close it had brought the two sisters, sisters who had always argued constantly.

'Birth partners?' Anne Marie smiled. 'Well, isn't that a grand idea.'

Birth partners.

Now, neither Anne Marie nor Roxy would be alone in the delivery room.

CHAPTER SEVENTEEN

If there had ever been a hotter summer Roxy couldn't remember it. Anne Marie became so heavy she could hardly bear to move in the heat. Roxy did most of her chores for her, though she had to admit that Mrs Dyce made sure Anne Marie hadn't much to do anyway, fussing round her like a mother hen.

At times like that Roxy felt guilty about all the horrible things she thought about the Dyces. Mrs Dyce was exactly as she appeared to be: a good woman, doing her best to help girls like them, risking prosecution if she was caught. Why look for something sinister when there was nothing else there?

Anne Marie was happy when Roxy thought like that. She wanted so much for her friend to love Mrs Dyce the way she did, but Roxy could never go that far.

'Have you told her yet that we're going to be birth partners?' Roxy kept asking, knowing full well that

Anne Marie hadn't.

'I'm picking the right moment. I know she won't be happy about it.'

Roxy couldn't understand what the problem would be, but she was sure Mrs Dyce would have an objection, one Anne Marie would agree with.

'You won't let her talk you out of it, will you?' And although Anne Marie promised over and over that she wouldn't, Roxy was still unsure.

Roxy grew tired of sitting around the house with the other girls, girls she couldn't talk to, who usually sat huddled together. And when Anne Marie would have her afternoon rest, Roxy took to wandering in the grounds once more. She was always on the lookout for Stevens. She didn't want to see him again. She had explored the house, and her curiosity was satisfied there. She knew more of Dragon House than any of the others. But on hot sticky afternoons, she wanted to be out, feeling whatever breeze there was in her hair.

It was on one of these afternoon rambles that she found an open gate. She had wandered up an over-grown path and suddenly, there it was, hanging on a broken hinge, with its wrought iron swirls of dragon tails and tongues of fire. Dragons were everywhere

here. The gate lay open and inviting, almost asking her to walk through. Had someone here forgotten about this way out?

Roxy looked all around her, sure that this was a trick of some kind and that someone, Stevens or Mrs Dyce, would leap out at her from the long grass and hold her back. She stood for a long moment waiting and watching. The path remained empty. There was not a sound, not a breath of a breeze, not even a crackle through the dry grass. She was completely hidden from view by bushes and trees. Somewhere in the distance, a bird was calling, but otherwise all was quiet. Roxy was alone. She stared out through the gate.

There lay freedom. The outside world she had been denied for so long. And Roxy couldn't resist it.

She had a feeling that as soon as she stepped through the gate the air would be clearer and cooler. There would be a warm wind and the shimmer of heat would show her the house was only a mirage and she would see a village, houses, civilisation. It would be as if she had stepped out of another dimension. But as she walked on the overgrown path, nothing changed. The path only continued through more long grass and trees and bushes. It seemed to be leading nowhere. She stumbled on, sure she had been walking for miles. She kept expecting to see some kind of road sign, but there wasn't even a road. Only this dried-out path. What would she do, she wondered, if she found an isolated farmhouse, or saw a village in the distance? Knock on the farmhouse door? Pop into a village store? No. There would be too many questions if she did that. But there was no farmhouse, no village. If anything the path grew denser and her face was constantly scratched by bushes, and nettles stung her ankles. She could be in another world. Roxy imagined herself in a distant alien planet, totally alone. Marooned, like Robinson Crusoe.

Finally, exhausted, she sat on the stump of a tree. So much for her foray to freedom!

She might as well go back, and she was sure she would find the way. She hadn't diverted from the path, she could see it winding back in the direction she had come, disappearing into the shimmering undergrowth.

Yet, going back now seemed like such a cop-out. She was free. It suddenly hit her that she was free. She could go anywhere she wanted.

She could go home.

Home seemed so much in her distant past that she could hardly remember it. What were her mum and

Jennifer doing now? In July? They were probably off on their summer holiday. Majorca. It had been booked before Roxy had run away. That was a lifetime ago. Yes, they would be there now, with Paul. Roxy could hardly imagine them cancelling it on her account. And they would have had her letter by now, telling them she was safe.

After a letter like that they would be able to go off to Majorca with a clear conscience.

Yet, thinking of them made her feel like crying. They seemed like people from the past, that she had read about. For the moment, her family was Anne Marie. My sister, my friend, she thought warmly.

Roxy patted her bump. 'And you, little man,' she whispered. She had decided for herself that her baby would be a boy. 'You're all the family I need.'

Her clothes were sticking to her in the heat and she was desperate for something to drink. She would have brought some water with her if she'd known she was going trekking. It was time to go back, she decided. Her long thick curls were only making things worse and not for the first time this summer she thought about cutting them off.

Anne Marie had objected strongly when she had

suggested it. 'You can't do that, Roxy,' she had said. 'Your hair says so much about you. You just wouldn't be Roxy without all that flaming red hair.'

Roxy smiled as she remembered that and she fanned herself with her dress, trying to get some cool air about her face. She closed her eyes and breathed in the scent of honeysuckle growing somewhere close by.

That was when she heard the music, drifting towards her from somewhere in the distance.

'*Summertime, and the living is easy …*'

It reminded her of her dad, playing his radio while they sunbathed in the garden, his last summer. There was something comforting and reassuring about music from a radio drifting through the summer air.

Nearby, someone had a radio switched on.

Roxy stood up and stretched to see beyond the bushes, but she could see nothing. She was too small. She began to walk, following the music like one of the Pied Piper's children.

The song finished and a voice announced what the next piece of music would be. A lazy instrumental began to drift through the sultry summer afternoon.

Roxy at last pushed her way through the under-growth and there it was. A silver grey Aston Martin

158

convertible, parked a hundred metres or so down a dusty overgrown track. Her eyes scanned the area; searching for the driver. James Bond must be somewhere nearby, she thought with a smile. Probably peeing in the bushes. There was no one to be seen, not a hint of a human being, but he must be close to have left the car radio playing. Roxy moved closer, as stealthily as her bump allowed. She felt almost guilty, as if she was doing something wrong. He'd be back any moment. Had to be. Yet, like someone hypnotised, she crept closer, straining her ears for voices approaching, twigs crackling, footsteps striding through the brittle grass.

She would be caught.

And then what?

What did it matter? She wasn't doing anything wrong. If she confided in this James Bond, he would take her to a police station. By tonight she could be home. Always, just when she was sure she had put home behind her, it was the first thing that came to her mind. Home.

The music finished and the announcer began a summary of the news. It had been so long since Roxy had heard any news that she listened intently. There had been a train crash in London. Several people had been killed.

Her mother and Jennifer could have been on that train, though it was hardly likely. But they could have been in some other accident that she'd never heard about. One of them, both of them, could be dead, and she didn't even know.

The thought made her head swim and she clung on to the car door for support. It was the heat. She had walked too long and too far.

A plane had been hijacked on its way to India.

She imagined her mother on a plane, a gun held to her head by some fanatical terrorist. Did they hijack package tours to Majorca?

The body of a young girl had been washed up in the Thames two weeks ago and had still not been identified.

That was the final story. And it chilled Roxy. Was her mother listening to that same bulletin, thinking, worrying that the young girl might be Roxy? Had she already gone to identify the decomposing body? The sudden picture of her mother watching, white-faced, as an undertaker pulled back the sheet from a corpse, holding her breath, expecting to see her daughter, her Roxy, lying there, made her feel so sick she almost vomited. How could she have done such a cruel thing to her mother?

Mrs Dyce was right. Maybe listening to the news wasn't a good idea after all.

A sudden idea came to her. She reached inside the car and pushed the button on the radio and the station changed from the old middle-aged sounds to the roar from one of the pop stations.

That would bring James Bond back pronto if nothing else would. Time for Roxy to be off. At the last minute she grabbed the newspaper that was lying on the front seat, proof of her adventure when she got back and showed it to Anne Marie. Now she had given James Bond two mysteries to baffle him as he drove off through the afternoon. Two mysteries he would never solve.

She wanted to stay and watch for his return. She wanted to see him look around, scratching his head and wondering who on earth had changed the stations on his radio and taken his paper. But there was nowhere safe to hide and see. And she was tired now, exhausted and thirsty.

It took her an age to find the gate again. And as she searched she wondered if she would ever find it and if she did, would it be locked?

And if it was, would it matter?

But at last there it was, still open. The dragons on the lopsided gate looking slightly drunk.

Yet Roxy hesitated before she stepped back inside. She was free. No one at the house knew where she'd gone. She could go back to that car, tell the driver she needed help. He would take her to a police station, and by tonight, she could be in her own bed.

She would keep the secret of Dragon House, of course. She'd never tell anyone about that. Not from any loyalty to the Dyces, but because of those other girls the Dyces were helping. The illegal immigrants, the asylum seekers, and Anne Marie.

Anne Marie.

Without Roxy, Anne Marie would have no birth partner, she would have to go into that delivery room alone. Roxy had promised her she would be with her. Anne Marie was like her sister, her best friend. Roxy knew then that she could never let her down.

It was because of Anne Marie she went back.

CHAPTER EIGHTEEN

That night Roxy told Anne Marie all about her little adventure. Exaggerating, of course, making it sound much more exciting than it had really been. In Roxy's version, the driver had almost caught her, and she had had to hide in the undergrowth while he searched around for her. When she'd found the gate, Stevens had been lurking there, and she'd had to distract him by throwing a stone into the distance to make him move off and investigate.

'I wish you wouldn't do things like that, Roxy. It could be dangerous. You don't know what kind of perverts you might meet up with. And you're so vulnerable at the moment.' Anne Marie stroked Roxy's bump gently. 'You've got two people to look after now.'

That only made Roxy laugh. 'Wherever I go, he goes.'

When she'd returned she had stuffed the newspaper

under the mattress and now she pulled it out dramatically.

'Look what else I got.'

Anne Marie jumped up and closed the door of their room as if they were doing something suspicious. 'You shouldn't have brought that back. You know Mrs Dyce doesn't like us reading the news.'

Sometimes Roxy had to admit that Anne Marie annoyed her. 'Goodness, what's she going to do, shoot me at dawn? I mean, it's a free country, Anne Marie. I can read anything I want.'

Yet, even as she spoke she realised she had sneaked the newspaper into the house, hiding it under her shirt hoping it looked like part of her bump. She had rushed to her room and slipped it furtively under her mattress. Every girl was expected to change her own sheets, so she was sure no one would find it there. Especially not Mrs Dyce. What had she been so afraid of?

'Anyway, it's not the news I'm interested in.' She said it to reassure Anne Marie. She held up the front page. There was an aerial photo of a derailed passenger train. 'It's all crashes and hijackings and fires. The whole country's on fire according to this paper.' Roxy opened at another page and a photo of a massive hotel fire. 'It says here because of the dry summer, places are going up like tinder. The firemen are on constant alert.' She flicked through the paper till she came to the showbiz page. 'I just want to read the good bits,' she said.

They lay side by side on the bed, catching up on all the real news they had been missing.

'Look, *he* got married.' Roxy was almost in tears at a photo of her favourite pop star and his new bride. 'I hate her,' she said.

'It won't last.' Anne Marie tried to make her feel better. 'She's on the rebound from that actor in the chocolate adverts.'

Roxy shrieked. 'And look what she's wearing! What was she thinking!'

It had been so long since they'd read any of this really important news and it suddenly reminded her of nights when she and Jennifer would lie on the floor of their room, with their favourite CDs playing, poring over pop magazines. Anne Marie noticed her going quiet.

'You should go home, Roxy. You've got a nice family. Mrs Dyce would arrange it.'

It had been a thought that had weaved in and out of Roxy's mind since she'd arrived here. As always she pushed it aside. 'Now I've got you, Anne Marie. There's no going back.'

She didn't need them, she added silently, and she told herself over and over that it was true.

Over the next few days she grew closer to Anne Marie than she had ever been to anyone in her life. Roxy watched over her friend, knowing her time was near. She hardly left her side. Anne Marie said she felt the baby had moved, locked into the position for birth. 'Ready for firing,' she joked. She was excited, but apprehensive, and she still hadn't told Mrs Dyce that Roxy was going to be her birth partner.

'I'll tell her. I still have a week or so to go yet, you know.' And she made Roxy promise that she wouldn't 'open her big mouth first'. 'I'll tell her at the right time and in the right way.'

But as the days grew hotter Anne Marie grew more uncomfortable. 'I'm fed up carrying this boy around,' she would say. 'It's too darn hot.'

'Maybe that's why Aidan's not coming out. It's cooler in there.' Roxy shouted into her friend's belly, now tight as a drum, 'Is that it, little Aidan? You're too comfortable in there?'

As if in answer he kicked against her hand. Roxy

pulled it back. 'The little devil. What a way to treat your auntie!'

Anne Marie said softly, 'You mean, his godmother.'

She took Roxy by surprise. 'His godmother? Me?'

'And who else would I choose?'

'Mrs Dyce.' Roxy had always assumed that was who she would choose.

'I love her to bits, but she's too old to be Aidan's godmother.'

Roxy, a godmother? It made her feel so special. She bent and whispered against Anne Marie's stomach. 'I'll be the best godmother in the world, Aidan.'

And she meant it. Oh, how she meant it.

There was a storm coming. They could all sense it. The new girls who could hardly speak a word of English kept praying as if some apocalypse were heading their way. One afternoon it grew dark and oppressive and the sky was slate grey and seemed to hang so close above the house Roxy felt she could reach out and sink her hands into the clouds. It was after dinner that night when the rain started. Great splashes against the window panes, and a wind that sent the trees outside swaying back and forth so violently it seemed they would snap. The thunder rumbled ominously above them, then cracked like a rifle shot.

'God is angry,' one of the girls said, crossing herself. About the only English Roxy had ever heard her say. She turned and said it again to Roxy. 'God is angry.'

'Well, don't blame me. I've not done anything to annoy Him,' Roxy said, laughing, but the girl didn't understand. She turned her face back to the window, her eyes filled with fear.

'It's only a storm,' Roxy said, trying to reassure her.

But it was much more than a storm. Roxy had never seen one like it. It lasted all through the night. The thunder would seem to rumble off into the distance and the air would grow quiet and still and then, suddenly, it would roar right above their heads as if it had sneaked back to catch them unawares. And there was lightning, every kind of lightning illuminated the sky. Forked lightning, ball lightning, sheet lightning. As if Nature had gathered all her forces together in one massive display just for them.

Roxy and Anne Marie watched it all from their bedroom window, wondering if it would ever end. 'Maybe God *is* angry,' Roxy muttered.

'He's got plenty to be angry about,' Anne Marie said.

'Murders and genocides and bombers. And people hurting children. That's the worst.'

Roxy agreed with that. No doubt in her mind. 'Yes, that is the worst.'

The storm reminded her of home too. On nights like this she and Jennifer would climb into bed together, snuggling close.

It was as if Anne Marie read her mind. 'Who says we'll push our beds together, just for tonight?'

The two girls lay long into the night, watching the storm, talking of the future, their future together with their babies, and hugging each other as close as their bumps allowed.

CHAPTER NINETEEN

The storm didn't break the heatwave. If anything the heat was even more oppressive next day. All the girls lay around the house, fanning themselves with magazines, too hot to move. Roxy had begun to notice anyway that the new girls didn't do the chores the way they should. The kitchen was never cleaned properly and the washing-up was always left undone. Yet Mrs Dyce didn't make a fuss about that the way she once had. 'These poor girls have enough to worry about,' she would say whenever Anne Marie complained about it. Roxy never did. She didn't care whether they cleaned up after themselves or not. She would be away from here soon, and she was glad of it. The house was changing, almost imperceptibly, the way a hot summer changes into autumn.

'I'm going for a walk,' she told Anne Marie one afternoon. The older girl was resting on her bed with the windows flung open to let in whatever cool air there might be.

'No more treks outside the gate,' Anne Marie warned her with a smile.

It was too hot for any real wandering anyway. Roxy kept to the shade of the trees as she sauntered round the house. Even in that shade, she could feel her dress sticking to her with perspiration. She sat under a big oak tree listening to the sounds of summer and wishing she had taken a book to read. Or even that paper, still wedged under the mattress.

She dozed off and dreamed of children giggling, her own child. She could see him clearly, a chunky little cherub pulling at her dress to stop her from running away. 'I'd never run away,' she kept telling him. She bent down to pick him up and suddenly, it was Jennifer. Jennifer when she was little and used to tag along everywhere with her. She was crying, and Roxy could see her face so plainly. 'But you did run away,' dream Jennifer was saying, 'and you left me.' She was crying and Roxy could make out her face clearly, every feature, her brown eyes, the bounce of her hair, the pout of her lips. Yet in life Roxy could never summon up a clear picture of her sister. Here in the dream she was as clear as a photograph. Roxy woke up feeling sad, missing her, wondering if the dream was a message to go home. That they needed her there.

Some hope. No one had ever needed Roxy.

She wandered drowsily back to the house and knew as soon as she turned the corner towards the sitting room that something was happening. One of the Asian girls was standing outside, looking excited, watching for her. Roxy began to run.

'Anne Marie,' was all the girl said, all she could say, but it was enough. She pointed upstairs.

As Roxy got to the top of the stairs Mrs Dyce was helping Anne Marie out of her room. Her arm was round her waist and she was carrying her bag.

'You're going to have the baby … now?' Roxy could hardly contain her excitement.

Anne Marie smiled and nodded, but at the same time she darted a guilty glance at Mrs Dyce. Roxy knew what that meant.

'You still haven't told her, have you?'

Mrs Dyce shot a look at Roxy. 'Told me what?'

Roxy wanted Anne Marie to tell her, but she hesitated for so long that Roxy couldn't wait. 'I'm going with Anne Marie into the delivery room. I'm going to be her birth partner.'

Mrs Dyce stopped abruptly. Her eyes went wide. For a moment, Roxy thought she was going to drop Anne Marie. 'I don't think so, Roxy,' she said severely, like one of Roxy's old teachers reprimanding her for doing something wrong. That got her back up.

'Anne Marie and I have talked about it.' Roxy looked at Anne Marie, silently begging her to back up her story. 'Haven't we?'

Mrs Dyce sounded angry. 'This stupid notion wasn't your idea, was it, Anne Marie?'

Anne Marie only shrugged. 'Roxy thought –'

Mrs Dyce didn't give her the chance to say another word. 'Yes, of course, "Roxy thought". I might have known it would be your idea.'

'It's a good idea,' Roxy snapped back at her. 'I'll be Anne Marie's birth partner and she'll be mine. I want Anne Marie with me when I give birth.'

'Indeed you won't!'

'But why not? Why is it such a bad idea?' At last Anne Marie said something. She sounded puzzled. Anne Marie, who never questioned anything Mrs Dyce did, was questioning her now, and Mrs Dyce didn't know how to answer her. She looked from Anne Marie to Roxy and said nothing.

She doesn't know what to say, Roxy thought, and she's making up a lie.

Right then, Anne Marie let out a low moan and slumped forward. It was just the distraction Mrs Dyce needed. 'Come along, dear. We've no time to waste. That little Aidan will be here before you know it.' And she began helping her downstairs.

Roxy stood in front of them. She had never felt so determined. 'I'm coming with her.'

'No, you're not, Roxy.' But Mrs Dyce's voice was softer this time and Roxy knew she had worked out her story. Worked out her story, that was how Roxy saw it. She would never really trust this woman.

'I know you mean well, Roxy, but I'm sure Anne Marie will agree that you're too young. Your own baby will be here in a few weeks. I don't want you going through two labours instead of one.'

'I don't mind,' Roxy said. 'I want to be with Anne Marie.'

Mrs Dyce drew in her breath so sharply her nostrils caved in. 'You're forcing me to say something I hadn't wanted to say. But if I must, I must.' She looked at Anne Marie. 'What if you have a difficult birth, dear. I'm not saying you will, but what if you do? Or what if something goes wrong?' Anne Marie looked so alarmed Mrs Dyce pulled her closer to reassure her. 'Nothing will go wrong, of course, but you must see that Roxy shouldn't be with you.'

Roxy butted in. 'If anything goes wrong she'll need me there to help her.'

But the argument had swayed Anne Marie. Roxy could see she had lost. 'No, Roxy, Mrs Dyce is right. You shouldn't be there. I'm sorry.'

Roxy couldn't help but be annoyed at her for giving in so easily. 'You promised me, Anne Marie.'

Roxy wanted her to feel guilty. But another wave of pain swept across Anne Marie's face again. Her fingers tightened on Mrs Dyce's arm. 'Please, let's get to the delivery room quick.'

'This is no time for discussion, Roxy,' Mrs Dyce said, pushing Roxy aside, almost roughly. She didn't lift her eyes to look at her. Roxy felt spurned as she watched them go, as if she'd been betrayed. Anne Marie was going, like Babs and Agnes and all the rest, and she'd never seen any of them again. She couldn't risk that with Anne Marie. She ran after her.

'Good luck,' she said and she hugged her and kissed

her on the cheek. 'You'll keep in touch, won't you? We're still going to live together, aren't we?' Roxy looked at Mrs Dyce, daring her to disagree with that. She still kept her eyes on the floor.

Anne Marie hugged her back. 'Of course I will. I'll send letters to Mrs Dyce and a picture of my little Aidan too.'

Roxy had a chill feeling in her stomach as she watched them go. She so wanted to be going with her. She had to know what happened to her. And in that moment she remembered that there was a way that she could.

She remembered the secret house, the rooms behind the table, that window in the dusty old library with the clear view of the labour wing. She decided then that even if she couldn't actually be with her, she was at least going to watch out for Anne Marie.

CHAPTER TWENTY

Roxy watched as the door marked PRIVATE closed behind Anne Marie. She waited only a few more moments, until she thought it was safe to move – why did she always think herself in danger? – then she walked unseen, like a ghost, past the other girls, already drifting back to their rooms or outside to sit on the grass. She walked calmly down the stairs, past the kitchen where two of the girls were arguing with each other in two different languages. Roxy was glad to be missing dinner tonight the way they were throwing hamburgers at each other. No one would miss her if she didn't appear for the evening meal. They would probably assume she had stayed up in her room in a bad mood, or had wandered off somewhere as she always did.

She stood at the place behind the stairs and looked all around her. No one knew of this secret place. No one else had discovered it. To everyone, it was a corner where furniture was stacked. Roxy crept right to the back and slipped her hand behind the table. She found the handle of the door and turned it quickly, praying it would still open, hoping she hadn't grown so stout she couldn't squeeze through the gap between the table and the doorway. She took another quick glance around to make sure she hadn't been seen, then she slipped inside.

The corridor was even darker and dustier than she remembered. A million specks of dust floated in the ribbons of light that streamed in through the shutters and Roxy stood for a moment after closing the door softly, just listening for any sounds. Someone in the shadows waiting for her. Stevens, ready to pounce.

There was still a chill in these rooms despite the heat outside, and Roxy shivered as she walked through them. She should be grateful for the cool air. Hadn't she longed for it for so many days? Yet it didn't seem natural somehow. It was like the cold air in a tomb.

You're thinking rubbish, she kept telling herself. But there was no disputing the fact, she didn't like the atmosphere here.

Maybe there were ghosts. That was why it was so cold. That was stupid too. She brushed the morbid thought away like a cobweb. Yet, why was there this chill in the air she couldn't explain? It shouldn't be this cold.

She made her way up the servants' staircase. Through the gloomy corridors she walked, stepping past old brocade curtains piled in corners, and upended chairs that blocked her way. Up the flights of stairs covered by worn carpets filled with holes and hanging loose on the steps. She had to watch constantly where she walked, for if her foot caught here she would tumble down and she couldn't risk that. Who would ever find her here? At last she came to the library. The musty smell of old books made her sneeze immediately. She remembered how she had opened one of these books and the pages had fallen apart, fallen into dust. Now she imagined them filled with maggots eating their way through the paper. Thousands, millions of maggots, here in this room with her, listening for her coming, waiting for her.

Why was she thinking these things? There was nothing to be afraid of here! Not here, in an old deserted library with dragons carved into the bookcases, and on the walls and in the roof. Dragons everywhere.

She had to hold on tight to the banister of the rickety

spiral staircase that led to the landing running above the library. Now, she realised how much fatter she'd become, how much more clumsy. She stopped halfway, exhausted, and watched the streams of light coming through the shutters on the alcove window. Roxy moved silently, tiptoeing, as if someone might leap out and catch her, as if someone might be listening for her in the deserted rooms.

The shutters were stiff, but she pulled and tugged and almost fell back as they creaked free. The sunlight burst in, sending an explosion of dust into the air. Roxy drew nearer and looked out of the window. There seemed to be no activity in the delivery room. But even now Anne Marie would be in there. Even now little Aidan would be pushing his way into the world.

Little Aidan, her godson. She flopped on to the wooden window seat angrily. She should be in there with Anne Marie right now, helping her, supporting her. Mrs Dyce had no right to stop her, no matter how 'logical' her reasons might be.

Roxy had wanted so much to share that birth with Anne Marie. She wouldn't have been afraid, no matter what Mrs Dyce might think. She peered closer but it was impossible to see anything through the windows.

What was happening now? How long would it take? Hang in there, Anne Marie, thought Roxy. I'm with you in spirit, I promise.

How long did she sit there, sweat trickling down her back from the hot sun, watching rabbits scurrying up trees and squirrels scampering along branches? Waiting for some sign that it was all over.

It was twilight when an ambulance arrived, a private ambulance parking close to the entrance of the delivery room. Roxy had almost been snoozing when she heard the wheels crunching on the gravel. It seemed to her the ambulance was so silent she was sure the engine had been turned off. She was alert in an instant.

The white-coated driver stepped out of the van and hurried into the delivery room. There was an urgency in his step that worried Roxy. Minutes later he reappeared with Mr Dyce. They were carrying a stretcher with a comatose Anne Marie lying in it. Roxy could just see her face as she was slid inside the ambulance. Why was she asleep? Was she so exhausted? Roxy felt herself tingling with excitement. She watched impatiently, because any minute now, little Aidan, her little godson, would be carried out, wrapped tight in a blanket. Or perhaps he would be in a tiny bassinet. She pressed herself close to the window to watch. Mr Dyce spoke to the driver for a moment, and then, the driver turned and closed the back doors of the ambulance.

Roxy felt like shouting. Why were they sending Anne Marie away without her baby? The driver got back into the van, and Mr Dyce slapped the doors. He watched the van move off before he disappeared back inside the delivery room. Now, Roxy began to panic.

Where was Anne Marie's baby?!

Roxy almost leapt from the window seat. Where *was* Anne Marie's baby? There was no way Anne Marie would have agreed to being separated from Aidan. She would have died first. Roxy ran in a fever, down the rickety stairs of the library, her footsteps echoing into the silence. She pounded along the corridors, not caring who heard her, blitzing her way through the long halls, sending dust flying, her footsteps the only sound breaking the eerie silence.

She stopped for a moment to catch her breath. The Dyces could have no explanation for this. She would not be fobbed off with another lame, 'logical' excuse. She owed it to Anne Marie, and her baby. Oh, how she wished she had insisted on going into the delivery room with Anne Marie. Her mind was ablaze with anger at herself as she ran back into the main house. She pulled open the door and slid back in front of the table, almost knocking it over, not caring now how much noise she made, or who heard her. She held her bump in front of her as if to protect it. Yet still the house seemed quiet as if no one else was there at all, except herself.

The smell of spices and garlic from the evening meal still lingered in the air. She wanted to tell the other girls, wanted someone to talk to, but none of them spoke English. She had no one to confide in.

The tables had turned. When she first came here, they were the ones left out of any conversation. Now it was her.

She ran to the door of the Dyces' apartments, marked PRIVATE, and thought once again, with a chill in her heart, that when you walked through that door you were never seen again.

'Mrs Dyce!' She yelled it so loud it was more like a scream. 'Mrs Dyce, open this door!'

She wanted to crumple to the ground, but she wouldn't. She would be strong, for Anne Marie and Aidan.

It was Mr Dyce who opened the door. He let out a

gasp when he saw her and bent down and tried to put his arms around her. Roxy shrank back from him.

'My dear,' he called back into the room. 'Come and help me. It's Roxy.'

Roxy stepped away from him clumsily. 'Where's Anne Marie's baby?'

His face paled. 'What?'

'I saw Anne Marie go off in an ambulance.' She was talking through gasps of breath, almost panicking, but she would have an answer. 'But not her baby. Not Aidan.' And this time her voice was a scream. 'Where's Anne Marie's baby?!'

The door was suddenly hauled wider and Mrs Dyce stood there, all in white, straight from the delivery room. 'You saw Anne Marie … where were you?'

Roxy ignored that. Wouldn't have told her anyway. 'I saw her, and I know the baby wasn't with her, and Anne Marie wouldn't have gone anywhere without her baby.'

Mrs Dyce took her arm, she was trying to lead her inside that room. Roxy pulled back from her with all the strength she had. No. She wouldn't go in there.

Abandon hope all ye who enter here.

The words leapt into her mind unbidden, like a warning.

Yet Mrs Dyce's voice couldn't have been more soothing and gentle. 'Please come in while we talk to you.'

Roxy shook her head. 'Tell me here,' she said.

Some of the other girls had gathered at the bottom of the stairs, watching curiously. Not understanding a word. Maybe that was what decided the Dyces to tell her in front of them.

Their faces were grim and Roxy felt her legs go weak beneath her. This was bad news. Mr Dyce caught her and lowered her gently into the worn armchair against the wall.

'Tell me,' Roxy said again.

Mr Dyce crouched beside her. 'We were afraid there might be complications, that was the reason Mrs Dyce didn't want you to come in at the birth.'

Mrs Dyce sat on the arm of the chair, put a hand on her shoulders. 'You have to be strong, Roxy.'

Roxy felt as if an icy hand was squeezing her heart. Strong, for what?

'Anne Marie's baby is dead,' Mrs Dyce said softly.

Roxy began to shake. Dead? NO! Not little Aidan. She could picture his little hands reaching out to her. He was her godson. His mother was her best friend.

Roxy's throat was too tight even to cry. Anne Marie

had wanted her baby so much. The first person in her life who would love her.

No! No! No! No! No!

It was too painful to take in. 'How can he be dead?'

Mrs Dyce spoke as if she was holding in tears too. 'It happens sometimes. The cord goes round the baby's neck while he's in the womb. We did everything we could, Roxy.'

Roxy covered her ears with her hands trying to blot out the words, but she couldn't blot out the picture they created in her mind.

Mrs Dyce held her close. 'See, how upset you are. Can you imagine how you would feel if you'd been in there with her? Was I right not to let you go?'

Logical. Just as Roxy had expected. She was always so logical. But Roxy had some logic of her own.

'If you knew there was a risk of complications, why wasn't she sent to a hospital?'

Mrs Dyce had the answer all ready. 'As soon as we realised there were going to be complications, we sent for an ambulance to take Anne Marie to the hospital, but it would have been too late anyway. Nothing could have saved Aidan.'

Roxy leapt to her feet. 'I want to see Anne Marie!

Take me to see her.'

The girls watching looked at each other, as if they were wondering why she was going crazy. Roxy shouted at them, 'Anne Marie's baby's dead! Baby dead!' They looked baffled. She had seen those same expressions before. The picture came back to Roxy of the night Aneeka had screamed almost those same words, 'Kill baby'.

No one had listened to her either.

'No, Roxy. You can't see Anne Marie. That would be the worst thing you could do. Anne Marie sees you, and knows you're going to have a healthy living baby ... and her baby ...' Mrs Dyce didn't say anything more. She didn't have to.

'But she'll need me, someone to talk to. I'm her friend.'

Mrs Dyce stood up, put her arm around Roxy's shoulder. 'She'll get professional counselling in hospital.'

'But she won't have me.'

'She might worry even more if she saw you. In case the whole thing harms your baby. You must see that, Roxy.'

She couldn't stop the tears then. She cried for Anne

Marie, all alone in a strange place. She cried for little Aidan. And she cried for herself.

The Dyces had never done her any harm, they had only ever shown kindness to her, and yet there was too much mystery here in Dragon House. Questions that refused to be answered by their logic. She would not trust them. She would never trust them.

Everyone disappears, she kept thinking. One by one, they've all gone, and now I'm alone.

No. Not alone. Never alone now. She held her hands around her bump protectively. Here was the only person she could talk to now. The only one she could trust. Her baby. And all he had was Roxy.

She had to calm down, she told herself. If she panicked, if she lost control, they would lead her off, the way they had led Aneeka. So she stopped crying, and let them take her back to her room. Mrs Dyce sat with her until she thought she was asleep. She even made her hot chocolate. Roxy only pretended to drink it, though she doubted they had put anything in it. They had an investment to protect.

Because as she lay on her bed staring at Anne Marie's empty bed she was sure she had figured out at last what it was they were doing here.

Anne Marie's baby wasn't dead. She was sure of it. With a growing sense of horror she realised that they were taking the babies and selling them for adoption, whether you wanted it or not.

CHAPTER TWENTY-ONE

The Dyces had pretended to Anne Marie that Aidan was dead. How could they be so cruel? Anne Marie would want to die now too. Now Roxy understood why each girl was whisked away after she'd had her baby, whisked off to another place, with no contact allowed. They had told all the girls, the ones who wanted to keep their babies at least, that their babies had died, and it would be too much of a coincidence if none of the babies had survived. She tossed and turned the whole hot night. It was all she could think of. It haunted her dreams. Maybe, there was still time for her to save Aidan, get him back for Anne Marie.

But how? She was only fourteen. She was pregnant, clumsy and powerless.

But smart.

By morning she had figured out what she was going to do.

Now she knew why the new girls, the replacements, were either illegal immigrants or asylum seekers. First they weren't able to communicate with each other, or her. They couldn't share knowledge. What was the phrase she had heard a few weeks ago when she'd found the secret room?

'Economically viable.'

More babies to sell, especially if they could sell them all.

It made her physically sick to realise what it meant. They could make more money, sell more babies.

'It's as if we're just cattle.' She said it aloud. But she was alone in the room now, and the empty bed, Anne Marie's bed, only made her cry all the more.

She knew what she had to do. She would pretend to believe the Dyces' story and she would ask to go home. All innocence, she would say she realised now how much she needed her mother. They'd let Sula go home. So why not Roxy?

Home. At home she could tell her mother all about this vile place, she would go to the police and their horrific little trade would be stopped. And Anne Marie would get little Aidan back.

But first, she had to make the Dyces believe she was completely taken in.

She found Mrs Dyce loading up her car. The Morris Minor. She had trusted them because of that car. People like that shouldn't be allowed to drive a Morris Minor! It wasn't hard to make Mrs Dyce believe Roxy had been crying all night. She had. Her eyes were still puffy and red.

'Have you heard anything about Anne Marie?' she asked at once.

Mrs Dyce didn't answer her. She hugged her close. 'You look awful, Roxy. You must rest all day. I'll get the other girls to do your chores.'

Roxy forced a smile. 'Thanks, Mrs Dyce … I'll be OK, but how is Anne Marie?'

She was afraid of the answer. Anne Marie thought Aidan was dead. He's not, Anne Marie, Roxy thought. I'm going to get him back for you. But if she believed he was dead, she might just do something awful.

'She's sedated, but … naturally she's taking it badly. However, you'll be glad to know that her family are coming over from Ireland.'

Now, Roxy knew for sure Mrs Dyce was lying. All lies. Anne Marie hated her family. They'd never loved her. Aidan was going to be the first person who would ever love her.

But Mrs Dyce knew Anne Marie's story too. She had become a mother substitute for Anne Marie, who confided in her totally.

'I know what you're thinking, Roxy. All Anne Marie's talk about her family, never going back to them, how she hated them. I've heard it so often, but when the baby's born, or like now, when a tragedy happens, what's the first thing a girl asks for? Her mother. That's what Anne Marie needs now. Her mother. We contacted them first thing this morning.'

'And Anne Marie won't tell them about …' But Roxy hardly needed to ask that. Anne Marie would never tell anyone about Dragon House. Trusting Anne Marie would believe everything she was told by Mrs Dyce. How could this horrible woman deceive someone who loved her so much? How could she separate Anne Marie from her beloved baby? Even worse, how could she pretend that the baby had died?

The thought was so horrific, so cruel, that Roxy began to cry again. She couldn't stop herself.

Mrs Dyce pulled a handkerchief from her pocket and wiped Roxy's eyes. 'Try not to be upset, Roxy. You have your own baby to think about. When I come back from town … we'll have a long talk.'

Roxy's nose was running, and she couldn't stop the tears. 'I want my mum too, Mrs Dyce. I want to go home.'

Mrs Dyce held her at arm's length, looking into her tear-stained eyes. If only she could read minds, Roxy thought, and see what was behind the woman's blue-grey eyes. But then again … what if she could read Roxy's …?

'I've thought about it all night. Thinking about Anne Marie, thinking about her alone, and now she hasn't even got her baby. You said it yourself, when a tragedy happens the first thing a girl wants is her mother. I want my mother, Mrs Dyce. I want to go home.'

Mrs Dyce looked off into the distance. She was biting the inside of her lip, thinking hard. Then she turned back to Roxy and smiled. 'It will take a few days to organise. We have to be very discreet. You do know that, don't you?'

'Of course.' Roxy could feel her heart beating like a drum at the thought of getting away from this place, these people. 'And I'd never tell anyone about here, you know that, don't you?'

'I know we can trust you, Roxy. None of the girls who have gone home have ever betrayed us.'

Roxy felt an urge to hug her, stupid though it was. This woman was planning to take her baby, sell it for adoption, pretend he had died during the birth, and yet she felt irrationally grateful because she was sending her home. Stupid or what?

'I have to go now, Roxy, but I'll get it organised for you and we'll talk later. All right?'

Roxy could have leapt with joy as she watched the Morris Minor drive off. She would be home in a few days, and then she would blow the lid off this whole nightmarish little business.

She went back to her room though the sight of Anne Marie's empty bed made her cry again. 'I'll get him back for you, Anne Marie. I promise.'

She lay on her bed and to her surprise, she slept. She dreamt of babies, as she always did these days, babies hiding in the house, Dragon House with dragons lurking in every dark corner ready to lick them up with their long tongues. Roxy was trying to find them, calling out to them, while somewhere in the distance Stevens was coming after her, because he wanted those babies to plant in his garden.

She woke covered in sweat. The oppressive heat was always worse in the afternoon. She pulled herself up and considered having a shower, just to cool herself down. Her baby kicked against her, reminding her he was there too, and he was hot.

One of the other girls was in the shower. Dietra, she was called. She was a surly Asian girl who seldom smiled. Roxy hadn't liked her but now she felt that maybe Dietra was as scared as she had been. Roxy decided for once to be friendly.

'I'm Roxy,' she smiled, but Dietra didn't smile back. Roxy pointed to the girl's belly. 'Baby good?' She gave the thumbs-up sign.

Dietra still didn't smile. She watched Roxy warily as if she was going to jump her, then she pushed past Roxy and strode out of the bathroom.

'You'll be grateful to me one day, kid,' Roxy wanted to shout after her. 'I'm going to save your baby.'

Roxy knew then she really was alone. The other girls could do nothing to help her.

She felt refreshed when she came out of the shower and ready for anything. Back in the room she towelled her hair dry. When she heard a car draw up outside, she went to the window and watched. Mrs Dyce got out and opened the back door of the Morris Minor. One, two, three new girls stepped out. They looked bewildered, frightened, and pregnant.

More girls. More babies. More money for the Dyces.

'Economically viable.'

Roxy stepped back from the window before anyone could look up and see her. She had to put an end to this.

CHAPTER TWENTY-TWO

Roxy had to put on a face, pretend she still believed everything the Dyces said. Lull them into the proverbial false sense of security. They had to send her home so she could tell the world what was happening here.

She went downstairs. Mr Dyce was in the kitchen unloading fruit and vegetables from a box on the table. He looked up at Roxy and smiled.

'Hello, Roxy. You look very refreshed.'

Such a kindly voice, such gentle eyes. Santa Claus personified. Surely, she had to be wrong. This man wouldn't be a part of any plan to take babies from their mothers. Then she remembered Aidan and Anne Marie, and she knew she wouldn't trust him, for their sake. She smiled back.

'I had a sleep and a shower. I'm sorry I made such a fuss. I was just that worried about Anne Marie.'

'Of course you were. You've nothing to apologise for.'

Roxy began helping him with the vegetables. 'Lots of supplies,' she said.

As if answering her unspoken question he said, 'New girls. Asylum seekers thrown out by their families for bringing shame on them. Poor girls. How can parents be so cruel?'

Roxy wanted to ask, almost did, how did you find them? How did they find you? It was hard to keep her mouth shut and keep the smile fixed on her face. They had to believe she suspected nothing. Had to.

'And none of them speak English?' she asked casually.

Mr Dyce shook his head. 'Unfortunately not. Which makes it doubly hard for them.'

Doubly hard then to understand how these girls could find the Dyces. In that moment, Roxy realised that there must be many more people involved in this operation. This wasn't just the Dyces. It probably also involved the same kind of ruthless people who brought illegal immigrants into the country, locked in vans; desperate people willing to risk suffocation, even death, for the hope of a new life.

The idea made her shiver. This operation was perhaps even bigger than she could ever imagine.

Mr Dyce lifted the empty vegetable box from the table. He tapped her hand. 'They might not be able to speak English, Roxy, but just remember, a smile is worth a thousand words and it only ever says one thing: I'm a friend.'

Roxy smiled back at him. That's what you think, Mr Dyce, she thought. This smile is saying, I don't believe anything you say.

The house was buzzing with activity. More beds crushed into more rooms, Mrs Dyce dashing about barking orders. There was hardly a moment to ask if she'd done anything about getting Roxy home. Roxy finally found the chance to speak to her as she was carrying sheets towards Roxy's room. Two new beds had been put there already. All change, thought Roxy. She was glad she was going. The idyllic picture of the house when she arrived, like a girls' summer boarding school, with midnight feasts in the dorm, was changing before her eyes. Now it was becoming a dark place, sinister and forbidding.

'Roxy, my dear. These are your new room-mates.' She introduced the three girls, dark-skinned, who looked frightened and wary of both Roxy and Mrs Dyce. Roxy took no notice of their names, she'd never remember them, and anyway she would be gone before it mattered. She wished she could tell them that she was going to help them, but all she managed was a smile.

'Have you thought any more about me going home, Mrs Dyce?'

Mrs Dyce was putting fresh sheets on one of the new beds. For the first time she noticed (why had she never noticed it before?) that the sheets were worn and torn. Old sheets. And why is there never anyone to help her? Roxy asked herself, knowing Anne Marie would provide her with one of her logical answers. 'The fewer people who know about this the better, Roxy. The safer it is for us ...'

And the safer for the Organisation. She had already begun to think of it like that. The Organisation.

'I'm so sorry, Roxy. I've been so busy today. But I promise tomorrow you will be my priority.'

I could phone home, Roxy wanted to say, phone Mum, tell her to meet me somewhere. In London perhaps. But she said nothing, and kept that smile fixed on her face. She began to help Mrs Dyce make the bed.

'No, no, Roxy. I'll get this. Why don't you change your own sheets?'

When Roxy came back into the room carrying the fresh sheets, Mrs Dyce had gone. So had the new girls. The room was empty, and the hot afternoon had grown even hotter. The window was open and somewhere outside birds were calling to each other. It could have been an idyllic picture of a perfect summer day. Roxy was glad she was alone. She wanted to think and all she could think of was home. She had never wanted to see her mother as much as she did now. She wanted to talk to her, confide in her. Her mother would know how to get Aidan back for Anne Marie.

Anne Marie. The thought of her made Roxy's eyes well up with tears. How must she be feeling, believing her baby to be dead? She tugged the bottom sheet off the bed and saw something sticking out from under the mattress.

The newspaper. She'd forgotten all about that paper, stolen, so long ago it seemed, from the front seat of James Bond's car. She remembered with a smile how she and Anne Marie had lain across the bed and read all the showbiz gossip.

In fact, the showbiz gossip was all they had read

about. Roxy sat down on the bed and puffed a couple of pillows behind her head. There was a warm breeze drifting in through the window, but not enough to cool her down. She fanned herself with the paper for a moment, before opening it up and beginning to read.

There was that train crash again. Some politician had run off with a pop star. The plane that had been hijacked. So long ago, it seemed.

Had the politician returned by now? Was his wife standing by him? They usually did. Were they still negotiating the freedom for the hostages on the plane? Had it all been resolved peacefully? She was suddenly desperate to know all that was going on in the outside world. She decided then never to be cut off from everything like this again.

She began to scan the columns, reading all the other stories hungrily. The woman who had sailed the Atlantic single-handedly for charity. The fires that were springing up all over the country straining the fire service to breaking point. A family whose home had been built over an old mineshaft and one day it had simply sunk underground. In the photo they were all smiling, as if it was a wonderful joke.

The girl's body that had been found, and was

unidentified. She hadn't read that story either. It had made her think of her mother, being asked to identify that body in case it was her own daughter, Roxy. How cruel would that have been? But she read the story now. Remembering how she had also heard the same story on the car radio that day.

The girl's body, a foreign girl, probably mid-European, had been found floating in the Thames. Not a suicide. A murder. She had died with a stab wound to the heart. And the girl had just had a baby. There was no clue to her identity, except for one thing. A tattoo. A tattoo of a cobra wound around her upper arm.

In spite of the heat, Roxy's whole body was suddenly bathed in ice-cold sweat. She felt as if she was drowning in ice. Her head began to swim and she was terrified she was about to pass out.

A cobra wound around her upper arm.

Roxy had seen a tattoo just like that before.

On Sula's arm.

The body was Sula's.

CHAPTER TWENTY-THREE

Roxy felt as if she was going to faint. Black spots swam in front of her eyes. Her throat was dry as dust.

The body was Sula's.

No. It couldn't be. Sula had gone home to have her baby.

She read the story again, just to be sure. The unidentified woman had just had a baby.

Had they kept her alive just long enough to have the baby, so it could still be sold for adoption? And then when Sula was no longer necessary, no longer 'economically viable', had they killed her?

A stab wound through the heart.

Roxy had to get some cool air, splash ice-cold water on her face. She needed something to cool her down. But when she stood up her legs wouldn't hold her. They buckled under her and she collapsed on to the bed again.

The body was Sula's.

It had to be. A young foreign woman who'd just had a baby. A girl with a tattoo on her arm. The tattoo of a cobra.

And a stab wound through the heart. That was the picture she couldn't keep from her mind, that horror image of Sula lying dead … a stab wound through the heart.

Who would have done it? Mrs Dyce? She didn't look like a murderess. Efficient, businesslike and sometimes so gentle. She would have to be heartless to kill Sula.

But she was heartless, Roxy reminded herself. Hadn't she taken Anne Marie's baby away from her? Told her he was dead? You couldn't get more heartless than that.

But murder?

Or could it have been Mr Dyce? No. Not with those soft eyes and that soothing voice of his. Not Santa Claus.

But she'd heard of Nazi doctors in the concentration camps who had seemed on the outside equally gentle and yet they had lured their victims, gullible, innocent victims, inside the gas chambers pretending they were only going for a shower.

Just as all the girls had been lured here, assured it was a place of safety.

Or could it have been Stevens? Yes. Him she could imagine plunging a knife into a young girl's heart.

Poor Sula. She had thought she was going home.

Roxy lay back on the bed, still bathed in sweat, and closed her eyes.

She knew now they had no intention of letting her go home. She knew too much. Just as Sula had known too much. Her fate was to be the same as Sula's. They would take her baby and then … She let out a cry. Couldn't bear to think of it. This baby inside her had no protection except for Roxy. She couldn't let him down.

She swung her legs on to the floor. Sat up. NO! She would not allow it. She cupped her hands around her belly and whispered softly, 'They won't take you away from me, I promise. And they won't kill your mum either.'

She would get away from here, some way. She would escape. She would tell the world. Tell them of the evil that was being committed here in Dragon House.

In her mind suddenly, as clear as the sharpest photograph, she saw the gate lying open. The gate she had found that day long ago. The gate that led to freedom. She had once walked through that gate unchecked. She would do it again. Today. There was no time to waste.

She was still wobbly when she stood up. One of the new girls came into the room just then, and ran to steady her. A smile is worth a thousand words. So Roxy smiled at her. The girl was Asian, maybe Turkish, she couldn't tell, but she smiled back at Roxy and Roxy had a sudden urge to grab the girl, run with her, save her and her baby. But that would be stupid. The girl would panic, not understand what she was trying to do. She would alert the Dyces ... and what would happen to Roxy then?

A stab wound through the heart.

She pushed the nightmare vision of herself, lying dead, right out of her mind.

She still smiled at the girl. Her legs felt steadier now. They would have to be. This was no time to be weak. Roxy would save this girl, save them all. She had never felt more determined in all her life.

She could take nothing with her. Not a scrap of clothing. Nothing. She would have to walk out of Dragon House, calmly, exactly as she was. She smiled once more at the girl to reassure her she was all right now, and then she walked out of the room, and down the stairs. If anyone asked, she was going for an afternoon stroll. She passed the kitchen where Mrs Dyce was showing one of the new girls how the cooker worked. She didn't even look up. Mr Dyce was nowhere to be seen, probably shut up in the office working out just how 'economically viable' the new batch of girls would be.

Roxy tried to seem calm and nonchalant as she strolled out into the garden. She tried to stop her legs from shaking, wishing the sweat would stop pouring from her. It wasn't just the oppressive heat. It was fear. Fear they would catch her and stop her.

Only once did she look back. She turned as casually as she could, as if she wanted to see the house from a distance, shading her eyes with her hand. Dragon House shimmered in the late afternoon sun, almost as if it was alive, another player in this nightmare story.

Then she turned back and kept on walking, walking towards the gate, hoping that she would find it again, praying it wouldn't now be locked and chained and welded shut.

And if it was? Then she would climb, she decided. Nothing would stop her getting out of here. She'd always been a good climber. A tomboy, her dad would tell everyone. She wouldn't let her bump stop her now. No. Not her bump ... her baby. She whispered to him gently, 'You'll be a good climber too. I'll show you how.'

At least she wasn't alone. That was what kept her going. Her baby was with her, safe inside her, relying on her.

She wouldn't let him down.

She stopped for a moment, leaning against a tree to get her breath back. Had it ever been so hot? This had to be the hottest, driest summer she could ever remember.

But she didn't dare stop for long. Soon, they would realise she'd gone and they would begin searching for her. She had to be far away by then, through the gate, out into the countryside. Freedom.

The gate couldn't be so far now. She would surely have remembered walking this far. Had she come the wrong way? She pushed the long grass aside to make sure she was still following the worn path.

Suddenly, she saw it, and she began to walk faster.

But something was different, and her heart fell when she saw what it was. The gate was locked!

She ran the last few yards crying, and gripped the iron bars with both hands. She almost expected those dragon tails to curl around her fingers, hold her trapped there.

'NO!' she yelled, shaking the bars in frustration. If

she only had the strength to bend them, pull them apart, pull the gate off its hinges, break the iron chains.

She laid her head against the gate and cried softly, 'No.'

'Trying to get out, are you?'

This time she screamed and turned, flattening herself against the railings.

It was Stevens, looking dirtier and darker than ever, looming towards her. His black hair was wild and his eyes were hooded and menacing.

She drew in her breath, tried to think of a lie. 'No. Honest.' Her voice cracked with fear. 'I only came out for a stroll.'

'I told them you were too curious.' He was shaking his head, scratching his chin with his maggoty fat fingers.

'No. I'm going home soon. The Dyces are getting me home.' She said it quickly, breathlessly. 'I just wanted a last look round.'

He stared at her for an age. 'You're going home?'

Roxy nodded. 'Yes, I've asked Mrs Dyce and she said that would be fine. She's organising it now.'

It was as if a pained expression came over his face. He drawled, 'Is that what she told you, you're going home?'

He was shaking his head, and if Roxy had had any doubts they disappeared right then. He knew she couldn't go home, ever. They would never let her.

'You know what's happening here, don't you? You know they're not going to let you go home.'

Please, please, please, she was thinking, don't let me faint. Though the spots were there in front of her eyes and her heart was thumping. Fainting was what she wanted to do. She blinked to try to make those spots disappear.

'Yes, I am. I'm going home.' Because if he thought she believed it, then he might just let her go.

Stevens stepped closer and she shrank back from him.

'I'm not going to be a part of it any more,' he said.

For a moment she thought she hadn't heard him properly. 'What?'

'You're just a kid. Too young. I told them that from the beginning. I won't be a part of what they're going to do to you.'

'What they're going to do to you.' His words brought to Roxy's mind the picture of herself, knife through the heart, and almost made her pass out.

'I'm going to help you.'

Was this really happening? Was the one she had

been the most afraid of going to be the one who would be her saviour?

'You're going to help me … get away?'

Now he looked afraid. 'I'm a dead man if they find out I helped you.'

That makes two of us, she almost said, but she stopped herself.

'Please, please, please, help me.' She touched his sleeve, still couldn't bear to reach out to those fingers. 'I don't want them to take my baby. I don't want him adopted, sold. I want to keep him.'

He looked so puzzled she was taken aback. 'Is that what you think they're doing here? Is that what you think this set-up is all about? Adoption?'

She couldn't think what he meant. 'They're taking our babies and selling them … to the highest bidder. And then they're telling the mothers that the babies have died.'

What could possibly be worse than that?

He shook his head, and his eyes grew black and heavy. 'I thought you knew it all, but you don't, do you? No, girl. What they're doing here is much worse than that. What they're doing here is pure evil.'

CHAPTER TWENTY-FOUR

Pure evil.

Worse than selling the babies? But what could be worse than that? Roxy grabbed at Stevens' sleeve.

'What are they doing here?'

He looked at her, as if he was considering an answer. His eyes were a cold watery blue. 'It never bothered me till you came. Why should I care about all them others? But you're too young. I told them that right from the beginning. Too young.'

She tugged at his coat. 'Too young for what?'

But he was already shaking his head, his decision made. 'Better you don't know. Then you really would know too much.' He was suddenly alert, as if he'd heard a noise in the distance, a crackle in the long, dry grass. 'Come on, I'm getting you out of here.' He produced a heavy set of keys from his jacket pocket and he began fumbling with the chains round the gate, loosening them, unlatching them.

Still Roxy had to know what he meant. The words 'pure evil' chanted in her mind.

'You have to tell me what they're doing here.' She tried to make it sound like an order.

He pulled his arm free of her. 'No,' he said firmly. 'It would scare you too much. It's better you don't know. Safer.'

The gate at last creaked open. It opened so wide Roxy was almost sure it was about to topple over, but Stevens held it fast with one thick hand.

'You get away, follow the old worn path. It leads to an old dirt track, but I can drive along there.' She remembered it, she almost told him. 'Wait for me when you get to the road. I'll go for the jeep, come for you. Drop you somewhere. What you do then is your business. I'm not coming back here either. I'm out of this place, for ever.'

He pushed her roughly through the gateway, anxious for her to be gone. 'You've not got much time. When they realise you've gone they'll be after you. You've been nothing but trouble to them since you came here. They both hate you, do you know that?' She could have sworn his voice softened at this point, as if he was pleased she'd been that much trouble to them.

'What are you helping me now for?' Roxy couldn't understand that. Here was this man, the one she had never trusted, with his dark, sleazy looks and his frightening fingers, now the one who was helping her to escape.

'Because …' He seemed to search for an answer. Then he said, 'Maybe I'm just sick of what they're doing here. Sick of myself for ever being a part of it.'

She tried to ask him more, but he only pushed her away. He wouldn't talk any more. He had said enough. She knew as much as she should want to know, he said. 'Go,' he kept saying. 'There isn't time for talk.'

She heard him locking the gate behind her as she hurried through the long grass, heard him wrapping the chains round the iron railings once again. All the time, as she stumbled along the path, two words kept repeating in her mind.

Pure evil.

What could he mean? What could they be doing here that was worse than selling the babies?

The girls had their babies and they disappeared. If they weren't having them adopted, what could they be doing with them? What else would anyone want babies for?

One thought kept trying to sneak into her brain but it was too horrifying to contemplate, too incredible to believe. Yet, as she ran, dismissing every other alternative, it seemed to be all she had left.

They were killing the babies.

But who would want dead babies?

Her imagination came up with what seemed the only one answer to that question.

Witches.

Witches would need babies.

Babies to sacrifice. Babies' blood was pure.

The Dyces were witches.

That's why they took the babies. Under the cover of looking after distressed girls in trouble, girls with no families to worry about them, girls with no homes, no country to care what happened to them. They took their babies.

Took their babies' blood.

The Dyces were witches. Probably the leaders of a vast coven of witches. All of them needing babies.

That would be pure evil.

Roxy had to stop. The thought was too terrifying to

face. Too unbelievable. But what other answer could there be? She was shaking again. She clutched at her belly. 'Not you, my angel,' she whispered. 'No one will ever harm you. I'll kill them first.'

And she would. As if they were already there, coming at her, she lifted a stone, held it in her hand like a weapon. She looked all around her, as if she was expecting the Dyces to come leaping out of the tall grass, chanting, holding the cross upside down, dressed in black gowns. If anyone came near her ... anyone.

She would kill them before she would let them hurt her baby.

Oh, she had to get away from them.

Pure evil, every one of them.

She began to cry at the thought of Anne Marie and her baby.

I've let her down, Roxy thought bitterly. And Aidan too. I can't save him now.

She felt a stab of pain when she thought of little Aidan. Dead already. She couldn't save him. It was too late for Aidan.

Well, she wouldn't let her own baby down. She was out of that place now, and she was never going back. She was going straight to the police.

Could she trust Stevens? He was part of it, yet he was sick of it, he said. He was helping her, wasn't he? She had to trust him. She didn't even know where she was. Where was this Dragon House situated? If only she'd stayed awake that first day when the Dyces drove her here, watched for signposts, roadsigns, directions.

Then it struck her. Of course, she didn't stay awake. She couldn't. The Dyces had drugged her. The heavy sleepiness that had overcome her hadn't been natural.

She remembered in the cafe Mrs Dyce had appeared to be so kind, insisting on fetching her tea from the counter. Perfect time to slip a couple of sleeping pills into her cup.

Pure evil. She could see it all now. Planned from that very first day.

Nurturing her, feeding her, ensuring she would have a healthy, plump baby so they could take it and ...

No! She stopped again, covered her ears with her palms to blot out the thought of what they would do, what they had done.

She would never let them have her baby.

'Do you hear me? You're safe with me. You'll always be safe with me.'

If only she could find a phone and talk to her mother.

How she longed for the sound of her mother's voice. Her mother would know what to do. She had always known what to do. When her father was ill, dying, it was her mother who had kept them all sane and calm. Always there for Roxy and for Jennifer.

She leaned against a tree and cried. Great sobs she couldn't control. Her mother had never let her down, or Jennifer, or her dad. She saw that now. Beside them all till the end. Holding his hand, clutching theirs.

It was Roxy who had let her mother down, and, she realised this, the hardest thing of all to face, she had let her father down too. Using him as her excuse for all her bad behaviour.

'I'll make it up to you, Mum,' she said silently. 'If I ever get home. If I stay alive.'

She stood up straight. She would stay alive. She had to. If she died, so would her baby. And he was going to live.

At last she found the road. The horizon shimmered in the heat and she was feeling light-headed, desperately needing something to drink. She should have brought some water at least. Her throat was parched and her brow ran with perspiration. Where was this place? Once again she felt as if she was in some other dimension. Some other world. Some other country. She found some shade beside bushes and fanned herself with dock leaves.

Witches. Could there really be witches in this day and age? She'd thought they only existed in books or in legend. But real-life witches?

No.

Yet it was the only answer.

She'd read a book once, her mother had brought it home from the library. It was about witches. Witches in modern-day Manhattan. *Rosemary's Baby*.

Rosemary had thought they had wanted her baby as a sacrifice, but actually, if Roxy remembered correctly, Rosemary's baby was the devil himself.

Rosemary had tried to escape them, she had done everything to get away from them, but in the end it had been no use. Rosemary couldn't escape.

Roxy hadn't liked the ending. She had wanted Rosemary to turn the tables on the witches, win out over them, go home to her family with her baby.

She realised too that was the ending she wanted for herself.

Her baby wasn't the devil. They didn't want her baby to worship. Her baby was expendable. All they wanted was his pure blood.

His pure, innocent blood.

Evil. They were evil.

She was breathing so hard she began to feel faint again. She wanted to sit down, but there was nowhere to sit, except on the ground. No handy tree trunk, no grassy knoll. She began drawing in long breaths, patting her stomach, murmuring softly to her baby. 'How are you doing, sweetheart? Your mum's shattered, but she's hanging in there, don't you worry.'

The sound of a car engine in the distance made her jump. She stood straight, almost on tiptoe and shielded her eyes with her hand to scan the horizon. The old jeep blurred into view, bumping and rolling over the rocky road.

It was going to be OK, she thought. He's coming for us. He kept his word.

'We're going to be all right,' she whispered.

She stayed in the long grass watching the jeep's advance. It was only at the last moment she saw who was driving.

Not Stevens.

Mrs Dyce.

CHAPTER TWENTY-FIVE

Mrs Dyce.

Roxy could see her eyes, narrowed as they searched the road for her. She looked around for somewhere to hide, to run. But the trees were too far, the road behind her too long. They would catch her. She couldn't think straight, she just stood and stared at the oncoming vehicle, bumping and rattling its way towards her. She was like a rabbit caught in the headlights.

At the last moment, she shook herself free. No! She would not be caught by them. She knew now what that meant for her, and for her baby. Mr Dyce was there too, sitting in the passenger seat. He held the door open, ready to leap out after her.

They caught sight of her at that last moment. He shouted out of the window at her. 'Roxy, my dear, we mean you no harm. We're taking you home, to your family.'

His voice was still full of kindness, so warm, she might almost have believed him.

But kind, gentle Mr Dyce was evil. They had no intention of taking her home.

'You can't surely believe anything Stevens said?'

Had Stevens betrayed her? Run to them as soon as he went back to Dragon House? Somehow, she didn't think so. Stevens was strong enough to have forced her to come back with him, dragging her all the way. And even without any violence, he could have come back for her in the jeep, and taken her back to them. She would have given him no trouble, trusting him until it was too late. She would only realise the road was leading her back to Dragon House when it went back through those ominous dragon gates.

No, they had caught Stevens, and who knew what had happened to him?

She had to save herself. Roxy began to run. Exhausted as she was, she put on a burst of speed that took her by surprise. She made for the trees, the only shelter she saw. She hoped she could lose herself in them. She hoped she could get to them in time.

She pounded towards those trees, trying to block out the sound of Mr Dyce's footsteps as they seemed to come closer and closer, crackling through the grass. Behind her too she heard the jeep screech to a halt. A door slammed. Mrs Dyce was after her now too.

Roxy's legs ached, but still she ran. If there had been any hope in screaming she would have screamed till her lungs burst. But that would only be a waste of what energy she had. There was no one to hear her. If she could make those trees, that shelter, she might be able to hide from them. Yet the trees seemed to be moving farther away. She felt as if she was running in a dream. Even the Dyces' voices seemed distant and dreamlike. Surely, she prayed as she had never prayed, surely she wouldn't be caught now. Not now, when she was so close to freedom.

She could hear Mr Dyce's laboured breathing behind her. She was running fast, even for him. He was too close, but he was tired and hot too.

'Roxy,' he was calling to her, 'Stevens is a bad man, you can't believe what he told you. We'd just fired him. He would have told you anything to harm us.'

They didn't know about the newspaper, didn't know that she knew about Sula.

Yes, she believed Stevens, now more than ever.

Pure evil. Witches, every one.

The thought of them chanting around her and her baby helped her to put on an extra spurt of energy. She would make the trees. Even lumbering and pregnant she would still beat Dyce.

She wasted no breath answering him. Hardly had any breath anyway.

'Roxy,' he was shouting now, as he saw Roxy was almost there, almost away from him.

She leapt towards the trees, and began to push through them, grateful for the cool shade and the darkness.

It was only when she was hidden by the trees that she allowed herself to pause for a moment, backing against the trunk, daring to take a glance back at Dyce. She caught sight of him through the branches. He stood with his hands on his knees as he struggled to get his breath back. 'Roxy!' He looked all around, still calling her name, softly, gently, pretending concern.

Roxy let out a long sigh, and sank back against the trunk. A moment, she needed only a moment to get her breath back. Then, she would run again.

Suddenly, her arm was caught as in a vice. Powerful hands gripped her and held her tight.

'What made you think you could ever get away from us?'

There was no pretence of concern, no gentleness in this voice. It was Mrs Dyce.

It was HIM who drove them back to Dragon House. She would never call him Mr Dyce again. When Mrs Dyce had grabbed her and dragged her back out into the open, Roxy had screamed and kicked and scratched. He was standing watching as she came struggling closer. For a second, she saw those kindly eyes, thought that perhaps he might help her, save her from the clutches of his wife. Instead, he had lifted his hand and slapped her hard across the face and told her to shut up.

No. She would never call him Mr Dyce again. He was Dragon Man.

A feeling of total hopelessness drowned her. They had won. They would kill her now, take her baby. Drink his precious blood.

Unbelievable but true. Had to be. She had let her baby down and she couldn't bear the thought of that. She would rather die. Dimly, she heard them discuss her fate as if she wasn't there. As if she was a commodity that people bought and sold.

'We'll have to induce the baby.'

'It's too soon.'

'We'll have to take that chance. She knows too much.'

This couldn't be happening. Not in real life. Please, God, help me, she prayed. Help my baby. She prayed as she had never prayed before.

As the jeep bumped its way back through those terrifying Dragon gates, her heart sank like stone. She was back in their lair. Trapped. They drove up the long winding gravel drive, past the main house, and she knew with a shiver where they were heading. They were taking her straight to the delivery room.

Abandon hope all you who enter here.

This was it. Her last chance. If she didn't do anything now, she was done for. Her baby was done for. For his sake Roxy refused to let all hope be lost. Her mind began to race, searching out an escape. The jeep bumped to a halt. The evening sun shone red in the sky, still so hot and with no breath of a wind.

Dragon Woman still had a tight hold of her. If she would let her grip slacken just for an instant, Roxy would run again, somewhere, anywhere. She would not walk calmly and quietly to her death.

But where could she run to?

As if in answer to her prayer, she heard her father's voice. Her dad, who had so loved his mysteries and his spy thrillers. 'Just as you think the hero is caught like a rat in a trap, he remembers he knows something that the villains don't know he knows ... that he's left a message with the heroine, or he has a cigarette lighter that fires bullets ... and that's what saves him.'

What did she know that the villains didn't know she knew?

The answer came to her like a blinding light in her brain.

They didn't know she had explored Dragon House, knew its dark corridors and its nooks and its crannies. They didn't know she knew the world behind the hidden door.

She could run there. Hide there. Even if it only gave her a few more precious minutes of life for her and her baby. While there was life, there was hope. Time to think.

Dragon Man swung out of the driver's seat and pulled open the door next to Roxy. How could she ever have thought his eyes were kind and gentle. Now they were icy cold like steel. The scariest eyes she had ever seen.

She allowed him to almost lift her from her seat. She had to let them think the fight had gone out of her, that she was weak and submissive. What she needed now was a diversion, and she couldn't rely on someone else to provide one for her. She would have to create her own.

Once out of the jeep they would lead her towards the labour room. Once in there, all hope *would* be lost.

She leaned against the jeep. 'I feel as if I'm going to be sick.'

'I'll go open the door,' Dragon Man said. 'You keep a tight hold of her.'

He hurried to the door of the delivery room, searching through his bunch of keys looking for the right one.

Of course they would want her in there, locked away, before any of the other girls would see her, begin to wonder.

'I feel sick,' Roxy mumbled again. She didn't have to pretend too much. Her legs felt so weak they were on the verge of folding under her. She was trembling all over.

She doubled over, leaning against the jeep, her arm outstretched on the bonnet. 'I think I'm going to pass out.' Roxy knew she *was* pale under her suntanned face.

She crumpled against the jeep and Dragon Woman let her sink to the ground.

She called to her husband, 'Alfred.' His name. First time Roxy had ever heard it. Alfred, such an ordinary name. 'We're going to have to carry her. Come and help me.'

She took a step away from Roxy, loosened her grip for a split second. It was all Roxy needed. She didn't waste an instant. With every bit of strength she had she was on her feet, pushing Dragon Woman so hard she fell face forward on to the ground. Roxy ran. Dragon Woman was screaming. Dragon Man was yelling. They would be after her in a moment. But this time, Roxy knew where she was going … and they didn't.

She raced round the corner of the house, out of their sight. Two of the girls were sitting on benches, enjoying the setting sun. How she wished she could alert them. Call to them. 'Help me! Get out!' and together all of them could escape, beat the Dyces. But the girls only turned as she headed towards them, looking puzzled. One of them stood up and Roxy slowed her pace. She realised that the Dyces wouldn't want to alert the other girls, or alarm them. They wouldn't want to risk their 'investment'. They wouldn't chase Roxy, not here. Not now. Roxy darted a glance behind her before she slipped into the house through the French windows. Still no sign of them after her. Good. She made a dash for the staircase, ran round the back to the secret door. Her legs, her whole body, were aching, but still she whispered, 'Hang in there, baby. They haven't got us yet.'

She was breathing hard when she squeezed up to the upended table. Once behind here, she would be safe, for a while at least. She had to be. Roxy slid her hand behind the table and turned the handle of the door. She took one last quick look behind her, and slipped once more through the hidden door, just like Alice in Wonderland. She was moving into a different world. She had once thought it was like a theatre set – now she realised that was exactly what it was. A play was what they were living in. They were all actors playing a part, and the only ones who knew the script were the Dyces and whatever kind of organisation they were involved in. Her and the other girls were in a play, a theatre of horror, and witches were after their babies.

She pulled the door tight shut behind her. As she crept along the dank passage to the servants' staircase and she imagined shadows lurking in every hidden corner to scare her, she realised that for once she wasn't scared. Not of shadows. Too many real things to be afraid of. Here she was safe. Comparatively safe. For the time being.

The secret place.

She was still trapped. She was still in danger. Deadly danger. But at least now she had time to think.

'They're not going to get us,' she assured her baby softly. Inside she felt like a tigress, protecting her young. 'They're not going to get you. I'll kill them all first.'

CHAPTER TWENTY-SIX

Roxy wondered if they would be already searching for her in the old house. Perhaps they knew another doorway leading here, and after exhausting their search in the main house and the grounds, they would realise there was nowhere else for her to go. She imagined them going from room to room as sunset gold streaked through the shutters. In her favour, they had no idea that she had already explored these secret places. Places to hide from the Dragons. That was how she saw them now, as dragons, evil witches.

Could it be true?

Could there be real witches here, in modern-day life?

Yet what other explanation fitted the facts? What else could explain their wickedness? They wanted her baby, all their babies, for their coven, for their spells. Not just the Dyces, but witches all over the world. A universal organisation of evil. Witches and warlocks and spells.

She sat on the narrow servants' stairs and couldn't stop herself from drifting into an uneasy sleep. She had tried to stay awake and alert, but weariness overtook her. It was a fitful sleep. She was constantly jerking awake, sure she could hear them closing in on her. Maybe, she thought once, listening for a sound, hearing nothing, maybe they had given up. How she wished they would, but she knew that was unlikely. Roxy knew too much. It was more than they could risk to keep her alive. But first they would take her baby. Her poor defenceless baby who only had her to depend on.

And she was useless. No one had ever been able to rely on her. She'd let her mother down. All the time her dad was ill, what had she been doing? Out enjoying herself, pretending Dad's illness was too much for her to take. Well, her mum had had to take it, and so had Jennifer, and they hadn't made any excuses. She could see it all now. All her mistakes came back to haunt her as sunset sank into dark. She'd been rebellious, determined to go against every rule. She'd made new friends, dangerous friends. Why could she see it all so clearly now, here in a darkening staircase with shadows in every corner? They hadn't been friends at all, egging her on to do things she knew she shouldn't.

When her mother had needed her support it was Jennifer she had relied on. Her wee sister, Little Miss Perfect. Roxy saw now that Jennifer was indeed perfect. She was thoughtful and caring and never put herself first. She'd been a rotten sister to Jennifer. She'd let her down too.

And Anne Marie, and Aidan. There was nothing she could do to help them. Nothing. It was too late. She had let everyone down.

She hugged herself, aware of her baby snuggling inside her. She wouldn't let him down. Her last chance to prove she could do something worthwhile. 'You hear me?' She caressed her stomach gently. 'I won't let you down. I promise.'

But she knew she couldn't hide here for ever. What she was waiting for was complete darkness. Under cover of the night and a moonless sky she could possibly sneak out of the house, make her way through the gardens and climb the gates to freedom. The thought frightened her, but what other option did she have?

She'd considered everything else. Even sneaking back into the main house, into the Dyces' office, using the phone, calling for help. But what could she tell them? She didn't even know where she was. She had no idea where this house was situated. She could ask them to trace the call, but how long would that take, and did she have that much time?

Roxy gasped as she heard a noise. Footsteps? Somewhere in one of the distant rooms? They were searching for her, room by room, she was sure of it now. She would have to keep moving, she decided, and after a moment waiting for more footsteps and hearing none, she began to crawl up the dusty stairs silently, her ears alert for every sound.

She reached the hallway and she stood listening. There was no sound. The house grew silent. But she knew they wouldn't have given up. She was sure they would be here somewhere, closing in on her.

Her heart fell when she saw moonlight streaking in between slats on a window. There was a full moon. Another bright clear night. So much for her picture of escaping under cover of darkness. How was she going to get away now? Why was everything against her?

She wanted to cry, but she held her tears back. Crying wouldn't help. She needed to think.

She moved silently to the window at the far end of the hallway. She was almost afraid to look through the broken shutters, sure the Dyces would be standing below, looking up, watching for her. From one of the rooms in the house music played, happy violin music. She imagined the girls sitting there, feeling safe. After all they had probably come through, they thought they were safe now.

Be afraid, she wanted to shout to them. Don't believe anything they tell you! She remembered how suspicious she'd been from the beginning. Questioning everything. Anne Marie had been annoyed with her sometimes. Well, Roxy had been right to be suspicious. Everything the Dyces had told them had been lies. They had all been in danger from the beginning.

She was hungry. So hungry. She needed something to eat, to drink. Especially something to drink. Her mouth was parched.

'When this is over, baby, we'll have a slap-up meal. A big juicy steak, and Coke, and fish and chips and hamburgers and chicken and …'

At that moment she would have swapped them all for an ice-cold drink of water.

As she moved away from the window she realised she must be somewhere above the Dyces' office. They mustn't hear her. She slipped off her shoes. She should move as far away as possible from anywhere they might be. She shuffled back and stopped abruptly as she heard voices, coming from an open window below and drifting up through the still night air. Their voices, loud and angry. Not afraid to shout. Who would understand them? No one.

'We have to find her. She has to be here somewhere,' Dragon Woman was saying harshly. Yet her voice was as ever soft and husky. Roxy could imagine her striding about the room, fire shooting from her nostrils.

'I'll find her. I'll smoke the little bitch out.' This was Dragon Man. How could she ever have thought his voice was gentle? It was harsh and cruel and vicious.

Their voices were too close. One floor below her. She had to move away from this part of the house. Unconsciously, she moved backwards, not taking her eyes from the shuttered window, almost expecting them both, that Dragon couple, to ooze through and swallow her up. If only she could think of some way to bring help. But she was too tired, too hungry, too confused. She needed rest, time to think things out.

Back and back she moved, one silent step at a time, afraid to breathe, because if they heard her breathe they would know where she was. They would find her. Further into the shadows she moved, safer in the dark corner, where they couldn't see her. She stopped for a moment, listened. Nothing now. Were they already heading back into the old part of this house, knowing she must be here?

Her foot touched another bag of rubbish, thrown into the corner and left there. Roxy turned around to move it gently, quietly out of the way. She crouched down and clutched at it, afraid that it might topple over with a whoosh and a crash and they would hear that, and she would be found.

She reached out for it, only wanting to hold it steady, expecting to feel plastic. But it wasn't a bag of rubbish.

It was Stevens' body.

CHAPTER TWENTY-SEVEN

What stopped her from screaming? Roxy couldn't tell. She wanted to scream. Every instinct yelled at her to scream. Looking at his so dead face terrified her. His eyes were open, staring at her. Dead eyes. Roxy scrabbled away from him as if she thought he might reach out and grab her, drag her close to him.

They had killed him. He had come back for the jeep and they had killed him. Because they knew he had been planning to help her escape. That had to be what had happened. What other reason could there be for such evil? Now they had even more reason not to let her live.

She had to get away.

She stumbled as her eyes searched the dark corridor, expecting the Dyces to leap out at any second. They had been here at this very spot only recently. They had probably shoved Stevens' body here just till it was dark, and they could come back and dispose of it. They might return at any second, find her here and then she would be done for.

For a second she couldn't breathe. Panic. She mustn't panic. She had to stay calm, think things through.

How had they killed him? A stab wound through the heart like Sula? But she could see no blood. No wound. Yet he was dead. There was no life in those eyes or in that face. Drained of life.

She'd never seen a dead body before. She had refused to look at her dad. Couldn't bear to see him with the life gone out of him. Looking at Stevens, slumped on the floor, his eyes open but dead of life, she was glad of it.

Had they poisoned him? No, that would have been too slow. Did they have time to do that between Stevens leaving her and the Dyces coming back?

What did it matter? she screamed to herself, biting her lip until it almost bled. He was dead, wasn't he? Proof, if she'd needed any more, of just how evil they were. And if they found her, she would be dead too.

Witches, every one.

No.

Wouldn't happen. She wouldn't let it …

*   *   *

242

She hauled herself back from her memories. Here she was, still crouched in a corner, still listening to the sounds of Dragon House. But she wasn't shaking now.

Remembering had helped her to think more clearly, though she could not forget the dead man lying by her side.

Perhaps, she thought, Stevens had something in his pocket that she might be able to use. Keys to the jeep? Could she try to drive it off? Would she know how? She'd watched her mother often enough. And Paul could drive, so it couldn't be that hard.

Or a mobile phone? Even better. It would be worth a try to call someone. She might not know where she was, but if she could phone her mum she knew she would believe her. She'd get help, find her no matter where she was.

But where was she? And could she keep hidden here until help came?

When she thought like that she lost all hope. So she pushed those thoughts to the back of her mind. First things first. She would search Stevens' pockets and see what she might find. Could she do that? Put her hands in a dead man's pockets?

If she had to, she decided. If it was going to help save

her baby she would do anything.

It was harder than she imagined. If only his eyes were closed, but they stayed open, watching her, accusing her.

Every second she expected him suddenly to flash those dead eyes at her, come to life, in the dusk of that corridor. Reach out for her like a zombie from a horror film, grab her, pull her to him. She watched for the least sign of movement, a finger twitching, a rattle of breath coming from his lips.

No, no, no, mustn't think like that. He is dead. Dead!

Powerless to hurt her.

Powerless to help her.

It took her an age to reach out to his pockets. Her hand shook, her breath came in short gasps, but she had to. She swallowed hard, steeled herself to lean towards him and slip her hand into his top pocket. Ready to scream out at the least sign of a heart beating against her fingers.

A half-smoked cigarette. The stub of a pencil. That was all he had in there.

Now, his left pocket. She drew her hand out again in disgust. A dirty handkerchief, stiff and grimy. She threw it from her and wiped her hands frantically on her dress. It was even more difficult to go back into his pockets after that. But it had to be done.

She found a comb, and that amazed her. Stevens, with his hair always wild and unkempt, looked as if he didn't even know what a comb was. And a box of matches.

She now had to force herself to dip into his trouser pockets. Would she ever have believed she could do such a thing? But it was a waste of time. Apart from some loose change, there was nothing. No miracle find. No mobile phone. Not even an address book to give her a clue to where this house was situated.

Roxy sat back on her heels and cried. Why was nothing going her way? Now what else could she do? She knew she had to help herself, only had herself to rely on, but she was backed into a corner and there was no way out.

So what was left?

If she could get up to the roof of this building she could draw attention to herself. Wave a sheet or a towel, signal to a passing plane that she was in danger.

Stupid idea. How could she, eight months pregnant, ever hope to climb up on to the roof, a sloping roof, clinging on to the tiles, waving a sodding towel?

If she could only send up a flare of some kind. That's what they did at sea. A distress signal. That's what she needed. But there were no flares lying handily about that she could set off.

A distress signal.

A flare.

She felt the matches still clutched in her hand, and knew in that instant what she had to do.

It was as if a cartoon bulb had been switched on above her head.

She was going to make the biggest distress signal anyone had ever seen.

She was going to set fire to Dragon House.

CHAPTER TWENTY-EIGHT

A fire! Why hadn't Roxy thought of it before? This had been the hottest summer on record, the driest. Hadn't that paper said that forest fires were starting up all over the place? Scorched grass bursting into flame. She remembered the photo of the hotel fire too. The fire service were on constant alert. Nobody could ignore a fire. Nobody could miss it. Surely, Dragon House couldn't be so remote that a fire would be missed. But even if it was, a fire would give her just the diversion she needed to get away. This time she wouldn't fail. This dry old house, with its wooden floors and panelled walls and ceilings, with its ancient tapestry curtains lying around, and the broken wooden chairs and the worn carpets, yes. It was a perfect torch. It would crackle and hiss and go up like a firework.

Roxy began to get excited at the thought of what she was about to do. She would climb to the top of the house, to that warren of attics, and as she climbed, on each floor she would pile up rubbish and curtains beside windows, in corners. She would start the fire in the old library. All those dry-as-dust books would go up like tinder. She would drop Stevens' matches, setting alight to one floor, before moving quickly down to the next.

From room to room, from floor to floor, lighting a beacon, lighting her way to freedom.

What of the other girls? Surely, she told herself, this was their chance of freedom too. The fire would start far from their part of the house. They would get out. There would be time for them to escape and one day she would tell them all that she had saved them and their babies.

As for the Dyces, she didn't care what happened to them.

Witches and warlocks.

Evil. Pure evil. She hated them.

Her hands were shaking. Here in the dark with a dead body close by her, she was suddenly afraid of nothing – except failing her baby.

Silently she began her journey. On each floor she dragged as much as she could, stacking it together like a bonfire. At last, exhausted, she reached the library. Here she dragged curtains to one of the old bookcases that was crammed full of old dry books. She began hauling books from their shelves and the curtains muffled the noise of their falling. Dry as dust, they almost crumbled as they fell. Now was the moment. She checked behind her to make sure she had a close access to the doorway leading to the lower floor. She had to escape quickly, and be ready to start the next fire.

How quickly would it take hold? Too quickly, and she wouldn't have time to make it to the next floor. She knew this had to be the craziest thing she had ever done.

She would never do anything crazy again, she promised herself. Enough of excitement. When this was over she would live a nice quiet life with her baby. She'd never complain about being bored again. If she lived through this night, she could handle all the dull, boring days life would throw at her.

If she lived through tonight.

The moment had come. She struck a match, held it for a moment, its flame wavering in the dark. It was now or never. No going back when she dropped this. She took a deep breath and let the match fall from her fingers on to the curtains.

At first she thought it wasn't going to catch. She stepped back, ready to run, stopped when nothing seemed to happen. The weak flame flickered and then seemed to die. Roxy held her breath, not sure what to do. She moved forward to look closer. A little pall of smoke appeared from the folds, and then there was a hiss and a flash, and like a demon, the flame leapt into life.

She couldn't move though she knew she must. Something kept her there. Some fascination she couldn't explain kept her watching as the flames licked round the edges of the tattered curtains, like something alive. She had been right about the books. The flames reached out to them and seemed to eat them up in one fiery gulp. Yet, still she stood. She had to be sure that fire would stay alive, burn, and keep burning. She watched and it amazed her and appalled her how quickly it caught hold, and grew. As if it had a life of its own.

She had once heard a saying – it came back to her now with a horrifying clarity – 'fire was a good servant, but it was a bad master'. She'd never understood what that really meant, until now.

This fire was going to be nobody's servant.

Already, it was spreading, grabbing, snatching with

fiery fingers at every loose curtain and dry splinter, devouring every book, searching around hungrily for something more to feed it.

Now she had to get away. She shook herself free of the nightmare that held her, and began to move. She began running down to the next floor. Already the flames were after her. She threw tapestries and bags of rubbish, broken chairs behind her as she ran. She dropped anything that would feed that fire. Somehow, noise didn't matter now. Fire was taking hold. She lit another match, dropped it on another pile on the next floor, then another match, just to make sure, before running down the next flight of stairs. This time she didn't wait to watch. She didn't dare. The chase was on and the fire was after her. Knew it had a hold on her, that it could mesmerise her, transfix her, hypnotise her until it could feed on her too.

Down and down she ran, hurtling down the stairs as fast as her bulk allowed. There was no dark now. The fire was orange and red and seemed to have only one thought in mind. It wanted her. It wanted Roxy.

'A bad master.' No servant at all.

It would not be controlled or told what to do. It had come alive, turned into something terrifying.

Yet still not as terrifying as the Dyces.

Where were they now?

She was on the first floor, and already the fire was beginning to rage above her. Surely, the panic would have started. The Dyces would be running, hopefully too busy to even think about her.

Look for her.

Or were they caught in the flames on the floors above?

Roxy was breathless, exhausted, but she had to keep going. No time to stop, already smoke was following her, drifting relentlessly after her. She heard a scream, then another, screeching into the summer night. One of the girls, alerted, was now warning the others. Good. She wanted none of them hurt in this.

Part of her wanted to run out of the house then, forget lighting the last fire on the servants' staircase. She didn't need it. The fire was eating the house, growing stronger, chasing her, blazing with anger now.

Yet she still couldn't take the chance. This had to be the biggest blaze ever. One that could be seen for miles. Roxy gathered sticks and broken bits of furniture, pulled curtains from walls and pictures with their wooden frames, piled them high on the stairs, on the floor, leading down to the bottom corridor. She would break the window on that corridor and get out that way. Not through the door behind the table. It was too risky going that way. The Dyces might just be there, waiting for her. They would show her no mercy. No, she would make her escape through the window, and then it would be a mad race to the shelter of the long grass. She took a deep breath and prayed, and then she dropped the last of the matches, striking not just one, but two, three in her excitement.

She longed to get into the open air, fill her lungs and run as far from this house as she could. She would wait in the grass for the fire brigade to come, as surely they must. The police would be with them. Oh, how she longed for that moment. Ready for questions to be asked, and answered.

The last fire leapt into life and Roxy stumbled back from it, her heart racing, her stomach heavy. 'Soon we'll rest, baby.' She said it softly. 'Soon.'

The house was ablaze. No stopping it now. Roxy stood for a moment, fascinated, feeling the heat envelop her, the smoke reaching out for her.

She could hardly breathe. Her eyes were smarting so badly she could hardly see. She had to get out of here.

Now. A sudden leap of flame made her jump, brought her out of her stupor. She moved, looking around and wishing she had broken that window before she dropped the matches. Yet, how could she? The smashing of glass might have alerted the Dyces before she had the chance to run to any kind of safety. This had been the only way.

She ran to the window. It looked out on to the back of the house and out and on to the fields. She could make them out through the cracks in the shutter. She glanced back, expecting to see the fire rushing at her, searching her out with its tongues of flame, its licking fingers. Sending out smoke to weaken her first. She grabbed at the shutters, and pulled.

Nothing happened.

No. This couldn't be. The shutters stayed closed. In every other floor they practically fell off in her hands, dry splintered wood, weak with age. Yet here, when she needed them to break open most, they were jammed tight. Could she make it to the next window? No. The fire would reach there first, and anyway, would the shutters there give any easier? She was growing frantic, grabbing, pulling at them, ignoring splinters and blood, pulling with a strength she didn't know she had. She was desperate to survive, desperate to save her baby. Now she had another enemy. One of her own making. The fire. It didn't care who its victim was. But it must have a sacrifice.

Suddenly, she roared, 'It's not going to be us!' She yelled it through the flames and the smoke. She screamed it like a demon, and in that second the shutters broke open. She fell back, scrabbled to her feet, gripped the window sill to pull herself up and over. She punched at the glass with both hands. 'We're getting out!' she told her baby. 'We're getting out of here.'

The glass smashed, and though her hands were bleeding, she didn't feel any pain. She climbed on to the sill. The sky was burnt orange, it was like the brightest golden sunset. The air hung with the acrid smell of smoke.

'Please, let all of the girls be safe,' she prayed. Then she jumped on to the grass. Her dress caught on a nail, but she yanked it free and she ran towards the long grass. She could hear screams coming from the front of the house, in the distance, but they came from the open air. The girls were outside, had to be. She didn't stop running or look back until she was hidden from view, throwing herself on to the ground. She was exhausted.

She turned on her back and watched Dragon House burn. There would be nothing left of it. Already its blazing windows were like gaping red eyes. The roof timbers were alive with fire and the sky was aflame.

Nothing would be left of it. Good.

And in the distance … could she hear the sound of a siren wailing closer?

Surely she could. That couldn't be her hopeful imagination.

Roxy tried to sit up. Now she felt the pain, in her bleeding hands, on her raw face, in her aching back. She gasped as a spasm gripped her and held her in a vice for a moment before letting her go.

But she knew it would be back.

She knew then she had something more than the fire to worry about.

She was in labour.

CHAPTER TWENTY-NINE

No! She couldn't be in labour – not now, not yet. She wasn't safe yet. Here, she was alone – and she was afraid. She tried to stand up when another spasm of pain tightened its grip on her. What was she going to do now? This wasn't fair. If only the fire brigade were here now, instead of somewhere in the distance, wailing closer. Please, hurry. She fell on her knees as if in prayer, saw figures running frantically round the house, silhouetted against the fire. She needed help, but not from them. She would be back in the Dragons' lair if she stepped out of the long grass and signalled for help. They'd take her baby, kill her baby, kill her.

No, she had to stay here. The fire brigade were on their way, she held on to that. More than one would come to a fire like this with its tentacles shooting out, reaching for anything that would burn. Already the grass was on fire and the trees nearest the house were ablaze. She could feel the intense heat even here. Her doing, this fire destroying Dragon House.

Destroy it, then! she screamed silently. I want it destroyed.

She gasped as she saw Dragon Woman appear, trying to herd the girls together, trying to keep them from panicking. She couldn't do it and Roxy was glad. The girls couldn't understand what she was trying to tell them. The only thing they did understand was fire. The same in any language. They pulled away from her screaming. Then Roxy bent double as another pain racked its way through her. Coming so often? What did that mean? That her baby would soon be born? Not now, it was too soon. She still had a month to go. And not here, not while Dragon Woman could still grasp her baby from her.

She watched Dragon Woman look all around her. Was she looking for Dragon Man, her husband, or was it Roxy she still searched for?

As the siren wailed closer Roxy could see, even from the distance, the panic on Dragon Woman's face. No mistaking now. Soon, soon help would come. Help she could trust. In her sudden panic, Dragon Woman began pushing, herding the girls into the jeep. Roxy knew what she was going to do. She was going to get away before the firemen came. She was going to take as many of the girls as she could, protect their investment, even now. Take some of the girls for their vile evil purposes, take them somewhere else, to some other Dragon House and it would all start again.

Roxy had to stop that. But how? She was growing weaker with every contraction. She let out a low moan as yet another gripped her. Her baby, eager to get out. He would be here soon. But she couldn't let them get away to trick another Anne Marie, to take another Aidan. She wouldn't let them get away.

Dragon Woman was piling, pushing girls into the jeep, and the girls were fighting for a place, thinking it was safety they were going to. If she didn't think of something soon they would get away.

Roxy staggered to her feet. There was only one way to stop her. She began heading for Dragon Woman. The fire engines were close, so close they had to be here on time. But if Dragon Woman saw her, it would hold her up just long enough for them to arrive.

One of the girls saw Roxy first. She started screaming and gesturing wildly, pulling at Dragon Woman, pointing to Roxy as she staggered closer. Dragon

Woman looked up and her eyes flashed with hate and anger.

'You little …' Dragon Woman screamed at her, jumped from the jeep. She was coming at her, anger roaring from her like the fire. Roxy turned then and she began to run. She ran towards the fire engines wailing closer, but she knew Dragon Woman was faster than she was. Dragon Woman was after her now.

Then Roxy saw them. She could have screamed with happiness. Three fire engines, their headlights beaming at her, advancing like great red monsters come to fight the Dragons. She began shouting, screaming, waving her arms about madly. Still she could hear mad Dragon Woman closing in on her. Ignoring everything in her thirst for revenge on Roxy. She would kill her even then, somehow Roxy knew that. But Roxy was going to make it. Her baby was going to make it.

She ran into the path of the first fire engine. It had to screech to a halt as she stood in front of it.

A fireman jumped to the ground and ran to her, caught her just as she crumpled to the ground. He looked from Roxy to the woman running behind her.

'Evil,' Roxy murmured. 'She's evil. They're all evil.'

Dragon Woman threw herself on the ground beside

her. 'Where's Alfred!' she screamed at Roxy, trying to pull her from the fireman's arms. 'What have you done with Alfred?'

She would have shaken the life from her if the fireman hadn't pulled her hands away.

'What's going on here?' he yelled.

'Where is he?' Dragon Woman screamed again.

Roxy turned her eyes to the blaze, raging through the house. Sparks and flames rose to the midnight sky. Not a room, not a corner would escape that inferno. Dragon Woman followed her gaze and let out a roar like a wild animal. Roxy knew then that he had been in there searching for her. Was he still there now? Trapped in the fire. Trapped with the body of Stevens? Roxy had a picture of Dragon Man running, trying to find a way out, enveloped in fire.

'Alfred!' Dragon Woman screamed, pushing Roxy from her and running towards the house. One of the fireman was after her, holding her back, though she struggled wildly screaming her husband's name over and over.

Roxy watched her unemotionally. Well, she thought, at least there was something she loved.

'How are you doing?' the fireman asked her.

She clutched at his arm. Was there ever a face so kindly? Here at last, a smile she could trust.

'Help me,' she said. 'I think I'm going to have my baby.'

CHAPTER THIRTY

Even as Roxy lay there in the fireman's arms, Dragon Woman was trying to concoct some crazy story to explain a houseful of pregnant, foreign young girls. Trying to convince them that her husband had perished in a fire losing his own life to save Roxy, not kill her. A story to make the firemen and then the police (when they arrived) believe that the Dyces were caring, philanthropic people. Philanthropic. Roxy was sure that was the word she had used.

No one believed her. It was too late for the Dyces. There were no real explanations for the girls who clambered out of the jeep, frightened, bewildered, unable to speak any English.

'Evil,' was the only word Roxy had the strength to say, and then she couldn't say any more. Her baby was coming. And all she wanted was her own mother, there with her, to comfort her, to hold her hand.

Roxy's baby was born in an ambulance. Roxy was hardly aware of who was there or what was happening. She wasn't even aware any more of the pain. She was too overcome with a blessed feeling of relief. She was safe. She had saved her baby.

She had to wait two more days to see her mother. Two more days too in which she learned just how evil the Dyces really were.

Roxy knew then she'd been wrong again, as she had been wrong so often before.

The Dyces weren't witches.

There are worse things than witches.

Witches are a storybook fantasy. What the Dyces had been doing was real-life horror, worse than anything Roxy could ever have imagined. Whose evil mind had come up with the trade they were involved in?

When Roxy had been told what she had saved herself from, and not just her own baby, but all those other girls' babies too, she had hugged her son – this tiny thing who relied on her totally – close against her, as if even now the Dyces might reach out and snatch him from her.

The Dyces had been selling the babies, but not for

adoption. They had been selling them for their organs. 'Harvesting their organs', was the way the police had explained it to her during one of the many interviews she had with them. *Harvesting*, such a beautiful word, debased, abused by the nightmare use the Dyces had made of it. The Dyces were killing their babies for their organs. They had been involved in a black-market trade for babies' organs, sold by unscrupulous people for profit. Used for transplants, operations and research. And then they were sending the girls back on the streets to get pregnant again, so the whole nightmarish process could begin once more.

Roxy had put her hands over her ears to blot out the words, couldn't bear to hear any more. She couldn't take in the magnitude of what they had done, to Babs's baby, and Agnes's. What they had done to Sula's. They'd never had any intention of sending her home. She was an investment they could make money from again. The police assumed that when Sula had realised this, she had fought for all she was worth, and that had sealed her fate.

'And Aneeka?' Roxy had asked.

'We've found Aneeka,' they told her. It seemed that Aneeka had been at Dragon House before, had been told then that her first baby had died. Back on the streets, pregnant again, she realised too late what the Dyces had really done, and planned to do again.

They had taken all the babies and killed them.

'How does anybody kill a baby?' she had asked the policewoman who had told her the whole horrifying story.

'There are evil people in the world, Roxy. And this was a worldwide organisation. With your help we've tracked it to Italy, stopped it. These people were on the lookout for vulnerable young girls, usually illegal immigrants, migrant workers – the kind who have no one to turn to, no rights under the law – and then they made them believe they were actually helping them.' The policewoman had paused then, taken a deep breath, as if even recounting it made her feel faint, too disgusted to carry on. 'All they wanted was for the girls to grow strong healthy babies inside them, and when they were born they were taken away from them. It was a sick, evil industry, but you can pride yourself on the fact that you helped stop it, Roxy. Mrs Dyce and the rest of them will go to prison for a long, long time.'

Not long enough, Roxy thought bitterly. Too late for Anne Marie, and for little Aidan as well. That was all she could think about. How could Anne Marie bear this news when she heard it? And she would hear of it. It was in all the papers. And where was Anne Marie now?

'Did Mrs Dyce do all this because she'd had a baby adopted?' Roxy had asked, remembering the story Mrs Dyce had told her.

That was when she had found out the real truth about the Dyces.

'Oh, there was a baby, Roxy,' the policewoman explained, 'but it wasn't adopted. It died. According to Mrs Dyce, because there was no transplant available. It made her very bitter.'

Roxy leapt to her feet at that. 'That's not an excuse!' she shouted. 'They won't let her use that as an excuse, will they?' For Roxy had a vision of some clever lawyer getting Mrs Dyce off, and that old witch's smug smile as she left the court room, a free woman.

The policewoman assured her. 'No, Roxy. No chance of that. Nothing could justify such evil. The Dyces had been arranging illegal adoptions for a long time before they became involved in this. As far as we understand, Dragon House, as you call it, was chosen especially because of its isolation. Set up especially for its evil purpose.

And now it was destroyed, Roxy thought. And she was glad.

The policewoman went on. 'No, the Dyces were mainly motivated by money, lots of it. That, and a hatred for the girls they were dealing with. "Lowlifes", she called them, who were bringing more lowlifes into the world.'

Roxy had been sick then. Couldn't stop herself. Sick that anyone could look at her baby, her beautiful baby, any beautiful baby, and think of it as a lowlife.

Roxy cried when her mother arrived with Jennifer. She had so much to explain, so much to apologise for.

But as soon as her mother stepped into the hospital room she ran to Roxy and hugged her. No explanations were necessary. No apologies. And suddenly, Roxy understood that too. She was a mother herself now, and knew she would always understand and forgive her own child. Jennifer forgave Roxy too, immediately. The baby saw to that. She rushed to his crib.

'Can I hold him? He is gorgeous. Look at his beautiful eyes.'

They wouldn't listen to her mumbled words of apology. All they wanted was Roxy and her baby.

Roxy named him Andrew, after her father. How

proud he would have been of his little grandson, and Roxy swore she would set about making them both proud of her too.

Yet, if everyone loved Andrew, Andrew adored Paul. Clutching his finger with a tiny fist, gurgling happily whenever Paul would lift him. And Paul adored him too, and Roxy tried to accept that and enjoy it for her mum's sake.

'Papa Paul, he can call me,' Paul had said as the baby lay contented in his arms. 'I wouldn't want him to call me Grandpa.'

She liked him for that, realised as the weeks went on that she liked him for a lot of things.

When Roxy had first gone, her mother and Jennifer had almost fallen apart, blaming themselves for Roxy running away. They had worried about her, tried to find her – had never given up. Even when the letter had come telling them she was fine – oh yes, Roxy realised she had fallen right in with the Dyces' plans writing that letter – her mother and Jennifer had never given up trying to find her. In fact, the letter had spurred them on, had given them hope that she was still alive. But it was Paul who had held them all together. Paul who had taken charge of everything.

Her life was so different now. Back home, safe with her family. But what about Anne Marie? The police could find no trace of her. And Roxy gave up waiting to hear from her. But Roxy knew she would never forget her soft Irish voice and the friendship she had shared with her those months in Dragon House.

Maybe Roxy would never find out where she was or what happened to her. Perhaps, she told herself, that was for the best. That way, she could believe that Anne Marie had made it, that she had somehow been reunited with her baby. She prayed it was so every night. That Anne Marie was even now somewhere safe back in Ireland with little Aidan running about, playing and laughing. That Anne Marie would live out her days happy at last, with Aidan, the love of her life.

A NOTE FROM THE AUTHOR

I had just finished a school event and as I drove home I switched on the radio in the car. A young girl was being interviewed. I was so shocked by what she was saying that I stopped the car to listen. The girl was an illegal immigrant, vulnerable and pregnant and alone in a strange country. When people had offered to look after her, she had been grateful for their kindness. When her baby was born and they told her the baby had died, she had no reason to disbelieve them. Only later did she find out the truth, and the truth was the most horrific story I had ever heard.

Someone has to write a book about this, I thought in that instant.

Then I had another thought. Wait a minute, I'm a writer. Why don't I write a book about it? But how could I write a children's story about such a horrific subject?

Then I realised that this was happening to young girls, the girls I write about and for. And by the time I arrived home Roxy's story was in my head and I was desperate to write it down.

It wasn't an easy book to write. Part of me felt guilty about writing it as a thriller. After all, these things were really happening. It was a story too that made me cry. I still can't read the last sentence without a lump in my throat. But, this was Roxy's story, and she was such a wonderful character to write about. Roxy starts off as a selfish little madam, who thinks the world revolves around her, who thinks only about herself. Yet she ends up a tigress who will kill to protect that baby of hers. I love Roxy for all her faults and failings.

Most of all I have to thank Bloomsbury for trusting me to write this book based solely on the passion I felt for Roxy and her baby.

Catherine MacPhail